W9-BRT-824

His name is Evan Michael Tanner. He is thirty-four years old and he hasn't slept a wink since a piece of shrapnel destroyed the sleep center in his brain during the Korean War.

Tanner loves lost causes and beautiful women. The FBI has a thick file on him; the CIA taps his phone. And a super-secret intelligence agency wants him to be their man.

But Tanner doesn't want any part of it—especially when the assignment is saving the top man in the global neo-Nazi movement from a richly deserved death . . .

"Block generates nonstop suspense."
—PUBLISHERS WEEKLY

LAWRENCE BLOCK

THE CANCELED CZECH

A JOVE BOOK

This Jove book contains the complete
text of the original edition.
It has been completely reset in a typeface
designed for easy reading, and was printed
from new film.

THE CANCELED CZECH

A Jove Book/published by arrangement with
the author

PRINTING HISTORY
Fawcett Publications edition published 1966
Jove edition/November 1984

ISBN: 0-515-07913-8

1

For a crow, the cities of Vienna and Prague are just a shade over 150 miles apart. When one travels by train, the distance is increased by almost one-half. The railroad bed meanders west along the northern bank of the Danube to Linz, then turns abruptly northward, crosses the Czech border, and follows the Vltava River into Prague. If the train kept to its schedule, the entire journey would take five hours and eleven minutes.

My particular train seemed unlikely to meet its schedule. It was several minutes late leaving Vienna, lost a few more minutes en route to Linz, and spent almost a quarter of an hour more time in that city than it was supposed to. I had left Vienna by six; by nine we had still not quite reached the border station, and I expected it would be well after midnight before we arrived in Prague.

The delay did not bother me. I had spent the major portion of the past week purposefully wasting my time. If I had wanted to proceed directly, I would have flown from New York to Lisbon, spent a few hours there, and gone on directly by air to Prague. But it had seemed advisable to create the impression that I was a rather ordinary American tourist on a rather ordinary European vacation. I had, accordingly, gone first to London, then to Lisbon, then to Rome, and

1

finally to Vienna. I was to arrive in Prague this evening, where according to the itinerary I carried, I would be met by a government guide and conveyed to a recommended hotel. After a busy day touring the Czech capital, I would go on to Berlin by air, take another train to Copenhagen, and finish up with a few days in Stockholm.

Once in Prague, however, I intended to depart rather drastically from my itinerary. After I slipped away from my government guide, it would become obvious that I was not entirely the tourist I had seemed to be. But in the meantime my cover was safe enough, and looked capable of doing the one thing it was designed to do—get me through the Iron Curtain without arousing anyone's interest.

My seat companion was French, a plump little man about forty with a dark shadow of beard and very little hair. He wore thick glasses and a rumpled silk suit. On the first part of the journey he busied himself with some commercial magazines. I had the window seat, and I spent most of my time looking out of the window and watching the blue Danube turn purple in the twilight. The whole countryside looked like background scenery for a Strauss waltz.

By the time we reached Linz it was too dark to see much of anything. I propped open my guide book and began reading about the town. The man beside me closed his magazine, fidgeted a bit in his seat, opened the magazine again, closed it a second time, and sighed heavily. The longer we remained in the Linz station, the more restless he grew. Several times he seemed on the point of attempting a conversation, but each time he held himself in check. Finally, as the train pulled out of Linz, he offered me a cigarette.

In French, I thanked him and explained that I do not smoke.

"You speak French?"

"Yes, a bit."

2

"It is a blessing. Myself, I have no head for languages. None!"

I said that this was a great pity, or something equally noncommittal.

"I am from Lyon. I am in textiles. A branch manager— I do not normally travel. Why should a man who speaks only French be sent on missions to other countries? Eh?"

He did not wait for an answer, which saved me the trouble of trying to think of one. "Extensive revisions in our pricing policies. Certain important associates must be informed in person. But why by me? First I am sent to Florence. Do I speak Italian? I *thought* I could speak Italian, but when I speak they do not understand, and when they speak *I* do not understand. Next Vienna. Three days in Vienna. But I was fortunate. In Vienna and in Florence there were men in our offices who could speak French. But Prague! What do they speak in Prague?"

"Czechoslovakian."

"How formidable! I wonder if anyone will speak French. It is not merely the men one sees on business. But the waiters, the taxi drivers, the clerks. It astonishes me that such persons are not required to learn French—"

He carried on in this vein all the way to the border. For all the talking I did, it was hardly necessary that I spoke French; it would have been enough for his purpose if I merely understood it, and was willing to nod in confirmation whenever he came to the end of a sentence.

As we approached the border, he asked me my own nationality. I told him I was an American.

He studied me very thoroughly. "But," he said, "I can see that you are not the usual American tourist."

"Why do you say that?"

"Ah, because of your manner. So many of your countrymen come to Europe with an attitude of—what is it? Superiority? Yes, just that. They do not even trouble to

3

learn the languages of the countries they visit. What is their attitude? Let everyone else learn English. An incredible attitude..."

The customs inspection at the border silenced him. Meticulous announcements of just what was going on were delivered in both German and Czech, neither of which my worldly companion could understand. I translated the German for him, explaining that he was to get his suitcase down from the rack and unlock it, prepare his passport and other pertinent papers, and otherwise ready himself for customs check. When the announcement was repeated in Czech, he demanded to know its content. I assured him that it was just more of the same.

There were two inspections. The exit inspection on the Austrian side was cursory. My own suitcase was not even opened. Then we crossed the border, and the Austrian trainmen were replaced by Czechs, and Czech customs officials paraded through the cars. This second check was a good deal more detailed. When the customs men left and the train started up again, I noticed that a government railway policeman remained in our car. We had been spared the presence of such an official in Austria.

I glanced over at him and saw that he was looking at me. He was a big man, thick in the shoulders and thicker in the neck, with a flat forehead and close-cropped sandcolored hair. I avoided his eyes for a few moments, then glanced his way again. He was still looking at me.

I wondered why. There had been no trouble with the passport. I was sure they had my name on a list somewhere, but a brief customs check would not turn it up. By the time they had put two and two together, I expected to be hidden in Prague.

Unless, of course, they'd had advance notice that I was coming....

The little Frenchman was talking again, assuring me what

4

a pleasure it was to have me for a companion. The pleasure, I wanted to tell him, was all his. He dropped a cigarette upon the floor, ground it out carefully underfoot, and sighed again.

"I think," he said, "that perhaps I shall take a brief nap."

"Go ahead."

"I have not had a decent night's sleep in almost two weeks."

I had not had any sleep, decent or otherwise, for over sixteen years, so his lament made less of an impression upon me than it might have on most people. In Korea, a fragment of shrapnel found its way into my head and destroyed something called the sleep center. No one knows exactly what the sleep center is, or how it works, but mine, ever since then, isn't and doesn't.

I watched my little French friend doze off in his seat and tried unsuccessfully to remember what sleep felt like. I could not recall the sensation. But I did not envy the sleeping man beside me. With an extra eight hours a day of wakefulness, he might have improved himself in any of a number of ways. He might have learned German, or Italian, or Czechoslovakian. Or, for that matter, tact and civility.

I looked out the window, or tried to; all I could see was my own reflection in the glass. I couldn't read my guide book. The lights had been turned off just after we crossed into Czechoslovakia. I closed my eyes and thought about the old man in the jail in Prague, and tried to figure out how I would get to him, how I would remove him from his prison, how I would slip him out of the country, and how I could possibly manage all of this without getting myself killed.

After perhaps fifteen minutes of generally fruitless thought, the train stopped and the lights went on and a pair of tall young men in dark green uniforms entered the car.

• • •

5

My Frenchman was awake and chattering but I couldn't be bothered with him. The stop, I knew, was an unscheduled one. We were not due to stop until Ceske Budejovice and were still miles from that city. I looked around. The train buzzed with fear. At the front of the car, the railway policeman was talking with the two uniformed men. I could only catch occasional words, and none of them were especially encouraging. "American... spy... Prague...." And, as if there were any doubt, *"Evan Tanner."*

Evan Tanner was my name. It was also, unfortunately, the name on my passport.

"Where are we? Why have we stopped here? What is the matter with everyone?"

"I don't know," I said. The railway policeman had turned and was looking at me. I noticed that he had a revolver on his hip. So, for that matter, did the two men in green.

"What is this? Are we in Prague?"

"No."

"Then why have we stopped?"

The railway policeman walked directly toward us. If the window had been open I would have gone through it. But there was no place to go, nothing to do. I thought of the days I had spent pretending to be a tourist. Wasted, all of them. I might as well have flown directly to Prague. For that matter, I might as well have shot myself in New York and saved myself a trip.

"Your passports. Both of you."

I turned. His thick face was utterly expressionless. The Frenchman demanded that I explain what was going on.

"He wants your passport," I said.

"The idiot saw it ten minutes ago."

"I can't help it," I said. I reached into my jacket pocket and wished that it contained a gun instead of a passport. I handed my passport to the policeman and wondered if there was any way on earth I could bluff my way clear.

6

It seemed unlikely.

"And yours," the policeman said to my companion. For once I didn't have to translate. The meaning was obvious, even to the Frenchman. He produced his passport and the policeman took it from him. The two men in green uniform moved up and flanked the railway policeman.

He studied the passports, selected mine, shook it vehemently in the faces of the men on either side of him. "This is the man," he announced sternly. "Evan Michael Tanner, American. This is the agent."

And, incredibly, his hand fastened on the Frenchman's shoulder. "Take him away," he told the men in green. "This is the man you want. Take him off at once. We're nearly an hour late as it is."

The Frenchman didn't understand. They asked him to stand and he had no idea what they wanted. "You have to go with them," I said.

"But why?"

Because Providence has supplied me with the stupidest policeman on earth, I thought. But in rapid French I said, "They believe you are an opium smuggler. They intend to torture you until you turn in your accomplices."

That did it. His jaw fell and he began to shriek that it was all a mistake, that he was innocent. If the twins in the green uniforms had had any doubts before, their reservations were now forever erased. No man who made such a show of innocence could be anything but guilty. They dragged him from his seat and walked him the length of the car. The railway policeman followed behind with the Frenchman's suitcase and magazines in tow.

I could still hear him screaming as the train pulled away.

"Monsieur Fabre? I am sorry to have troubled you, sir. Your passport—"

I nodded dumbly, took the little Frenchman's passport

7

from the policeman, tucked it away in my pocket. My heart was still pounding and my hands were slippery with sweat. I did not trust myself to look at the man, much less speak to him.

"An unfortunate interruption. The man sitting with you was a spy, an American agent. A very dangerous man!"

The policeman sighed and eased himself into the seat beside me. I wished he would go away. He offered me a cigarette. I shook my head. He lit one himself, inhaled deeply, blew out a cloud of bluish smoke.

For several moments he was silent. I leaned back in my seat, closed my eyes, pretended to be asleep. When he spoke again, he switched from Czech to German, an oddly accented German with reedy vowels and softened consonants.

"I am no Czech," he said. "I am from the Sudetenland. You understand?"

I nodded.

"By now they know their mistake. They will call ahead to the next stop. Tyn. It is not scheduled, but they will stop the train there. You must get off before then. You understand?"

"Yes."

"Go to Pisek. There is a man there named Kurt Neumann. He will hide you and help you get to Prague. Tell him Heinz Moll. You understand?"

"I understand."

"You will help the old man? Help him out of this damned country. I'll go now. Wait to the count of twenty, then follow me."

He left. I counted to twenty, got up from my seat, walked after him to the rear of the car. I found him waiting on the trestle between the two cars.

He said, "Kurt Neumann in Pisek. You remember that?"

"I'll remember."

"I cannot stop the train. They would remember. I can

8

go to the front, talk with the engineer. I can pretend to see something on the track and he will slow down to twenty kilometers an hour. When the train slows you will jump. You understand?"

"I understand."

"Good." He hesitated. Then he straightened up sharply, and his right arm swung upward and his heels clicked sharply together.

"Heil Hitler!"

The words were sharp and clear over the roar of the train. I brought up my own hand in the familiar salute, met his eyes with mine, echoed his words.

"Heil Hitler!"

2

When the telephone rang to begin it all, I was sitting at my desk typing up the last few pages of an eight-page report which Diane Blumberg would submit as her term paper in Shakespearean Tragedy. The paper was one I'd originally written several years ago for an NYU student. Since then it had made appearances at Barnard, Adelphi, and Fordham, and now Miss Blumberg would add Hofstra to the list. It was one of my favorites, built upon the thesis that *Hamlet* was intended by its author as a comedy, a sort of farcical satire upon the earlier Elizabethan tragedy-of-blood cliché. The neurotically indecisive Hamlet, the accidental murder of the buffoon Polonius, the manner in which revenge is constantly thwarted by Hamlet's own incompetence—these and other elements combined to make a legitimate if un-convincing case for my argument. *Highly original! An unlikely but engaging viewpoint.* A-, the instructor at NYU at written. *I'd dearly love to see the play performed as a comedy,* said a professor at Adelphi, who'd given the author of record an A. Barnard and Fordham gave the paper a B, the former musing that the student didn't *seriously mean all of this, do you?* and the latter offering jesuitical dispu-tation but giving grudging praise to the originality and log-ical organization of the argument.

Because the paper involved no new work on my part beyond running it once more through the typewriter, I was charging Diane Blumberg $25 for it. Original papers come higher; masters and doctoral theses cost up to a thousand dollars. This is not terribly high, considering the time and effort I put into my work, but it is the sort of work I enjoy. The income it provides, added to the $112 monthly disability pension which the government pays me for my permanent insomnia, is sufficient unto my needs.

"...of incest as a humorous component," I typed. "Ophelia's madness and its sexual overtones, seen in this light..." And the telephone rang.

I answered it. A young man said, "Mr. Tanner? My name is Jeff Lind. A friend suggested that I get in touch with you."

"Oh?"

"Could I come up and see you?"

"What about?"

"I'm enrolled at Columbia. There's...uh...something I wanted to talk to you about."

"Go ahead."

"Huh? Well, I'd rather not go into it over the phone."

"No one from Columbia has a tap on my phone. At least I don't think—"

"Would it be all right if I come up to your apartment?"

"Not before noon."

"Well—"

"I'll be busy until then."

"All right," he said. I asked if he had my address. He said he did, and that he would see me at noon. I finished up Diane Blumberg's term paper, put it in an envelope, and went downstairs to mail it to her. I picked up my own mail on the way back and carted it upstairs. There was the usual glut of pamphlets and magazines and newspapers, a batch of appeals for donations, and a good bit of foreign corre-

12

spondence. Sir William Wheatly had dashed off an enthusiastic note accepting an article of mine for the quarterly bulletin of the Flat Earth Society of England. He liked my thesis that the sky was a curved two-dimensional entity. Rolfe MacGoohan of the Jacobite League reported sadly that he had made no headway with Prince Rupert of Bavaria, the Stuart pretender we hoped to restore to the English throne. A French anarchist named Claude Martinot sent me an elaborately engraved announcement of the marriage of his daughter Monique to a M. Henri Pierre Peugeot.

I had barely organized the morning mail, much less read through it, when my doorbell rang. It was eleven-thirty. I opened the door and admitted a young man with a crew cut, an NYU sweat shirt, chino pants, and dirty tennis sneakers.

He said that he was Jeff Lind, and I said that he was early.

He came inside, closed the door. Once inside his manner changed remarkably. He put a cautionary forefinger to his lips, took a folded slip of paper from his pocket, passed it urgently to me, put his finger to his lips again, motioned for me to unfold the slip of paper, and then began to talk rapidly about a paper he had to prepare for his economics seminar.

I unfolded the paper he had handed me. It was a single sheet of typing paper with this message on it.

TANNER:
IGNORE EVERYTHING I SAY AND MAKE NORMAL ARRANGEMENTS WITH ME FOR THE ECONOMICS PAPER. WE HAVE REASON TO BELIEVE THAT YOUR APARTMENT IS BUGGED AND YOUR PHONE TAPPED. THE CHIEF WANTS TO SEE YOU THIS AFTERNOON. HE WILL BE IN ROOM 1114 OF THE RUTLEDGE HOTEL. ARRIVE THERE AT 2:45. MAKE SURE NO ONE FOLLOWS YOU. DESTROY THIS NOTE.

The bearer of the note went on to explain the details of his economics assignment. Everything he said sounded as though it had been carefully memorized and laboriously rehearsed. We discussed time, price, and theme. True to my instructions, I ignored everything he said.

The Chief was a pudgy man in an expensive blue suit which appeared to have been perfectly tailored for someone else. It was tight around his waist and loose at his shoulders. He closed the door, motioned me to a couch, offered me a cigarette which I refused and a drink which I accepted.

"You'll excuse this morning's dramatics," he said. "Probably unnecessary, but it's unwise to take chances."

"Is my apartment really bugged? And my phone?"

"We think so."

"By whom?"

"Either the CIA or the FBI. Quite possibly both. The Agency boys know you worked for us. They're always hungry to find out something about us. The fact that we work better without their scrutiny doesn't seem to deter them." He shook his head sadly. "Sometimes," he said, "those Boy Scouts seem to forget that we're all on the same side."

"And the FBI?"

"They don't know of your connection with us. I'm not entirely sure whether or not they know of our existence, as far as that goes. But they have you pegged as a subversive, you know."

"They visit me all the time."

"Well, you *are* a member of a startling number of unusual organizations, Tanner. Your allegiances more or less blanket the Attorney General's subversive list." He sipped tentatively at his drink. "But that's beside the point. I told you last time that we might have a piece of work for you now and again. I liked the way you handled yourself, particularly

14

in Macedonia. We're still collecting dividends from the revolution you started."

I had met the Chief once before, in an unidentified office somewhere in Washington. His name was one of the myriad things about him which I did not know. He headed an extraordinary secret government agency, also blessed with an unknown name. I knew that he thought I had been recruited by an agent of his, a man named Dahlmann whom I had seen shot down by the Dublin police. I knew that his men went places and did things, that they were permitted an unusual amount of independence and were encouraged to use their own judgment and discretion. And that, actually, was just about all I did know.

"Something unusual has come up," he said. "Something that I think might be particularly suited to a man of your talents and connections. I don't suppose you've heard of a man named Janos Kotacek?"

"Yes, I have."

"That's not surprising. Very few people have. Kotacek was a Slovak who—did you say yes, you *have* heard of him?"

"If you mean Josef Tiso's Internal Affairs minister in the Slovak puppet government, yes, I have."

"Well, that's a pleasant surprise, Tanner. It should save us a great deal of time." He leaned forward in his chair and rested his plump hands upon his knees. "When Czechoslovakia fell to the Russians, Kotacek got out in time. He ran to Germany and stayed there until the fall. Again he got out in time. We're not sure where he went from Germany. Argentina, possibly, or perhaps Spain. He seems to have been active, though from a distance, in the abortive fascist coup after the assassination of Masaryk. Of course that never got off the ground—the Russians were in there and they stayed. A few years ago he turned up in Brazil. He was in touch, evidently, with much of the Nazi Underground. Is-

15

raeli agents almost captured him outside of Sao Paulo. He escaped. In 1963 there were rumors that he had committed suicide."

"That's what I had heard."

"Did you? Do you happen to remember the details?"

"Not clearly. I think he was supposed to have shot himself in Brazil."

He nodded. "That was one story. Another had him discovering that he was dying of cancer or some such, and taking poison. It appears he did neither. Instead he went to Lisbon. He lived unobtrusively but well. His Swiss bank accounts have evidently not yet run dry. Ten days ago . . . more whiskey, Tanner?"

"Please."

He filled our glasses. "Let me see," he said, "where was I?"

"Ten days ago . . ."

"Yes. Ten days ago, agents of the Czechoslovak secret police kidnapped Kotacek from his home in Lisbon and spirited him away. The day before yesterday they landed him in Prague and tucked him into a prison cell. In approximately three weeks he will be brought to public trial, charged with collaboration with the enemy, complicity in the murder of several hundred thousand Slovakian Jews and Gypsies, and a variety of more specific war crimes. He will be found guilty on all counts and will be hanged."

"Good for him."

"I think not, Tanner. Not good at all, for him or for us." He leaned forward. "We've known of Kotacek's whereabouts almost from the day he turned up in Lisbon. And we've been very careful to leave him alone. From his base in Portugal, Kotacek has been one of the key figures in the global neo-Nazi movement. As you may know, the orientation of Nazism has changed slightly since Hitler's death. Germans remain at the helm, but the *idée fixe* has shifted

16

from Aryan supremacy to general white supremacy. Anti-Semitism is still a chief tenet, but anti-Negro and anti-Oriental policies have come to the fore; integration and the Yellow Peril arc evidently more potent scapegoats. The movement aims at developing little Nazi parties throughout the world and making power plays in various countries whenever circumstances seem right.

"Kotacek, as I said, is at the hub of all this activity. It's probably no exaggeration to say that he is the most influential non-German in the contemporary Nazi movement. He has contacts all over the world. He engages in constant correspondence with open and clandestine Nazi leaders. He's one of the few men anywhere who know just what's going on among the leaders of the Fourth Reich—which is what they're apt to call themselves, incidentally—not just in one country, but everywhere." He paused, raised his glass, set it down. "He has been extremely useful to us."

"How?"

"He writes to a man named Ottmar Pedersen, a Dane living in the Bronx. Over the past few years he has passed on a great deal of important information to Pedersen."

"And Pedersen is your agent?"

"No. Pedersen is a loyal Nazi, a member of Madole's National Renaissance Party. The man who opens Pedersen's mail is our agent."

"I see."

He got to his feet. "Kotacek knows a great deal more than he has ever told or will ever tell to Pedersen. At one time we considered killing our Golden Goose—making a raid on Kotacek's home in Lisbon and grabbing off what records we could. This was always rejected. The information is only valuable when our knowledge of it is not known. Sooner or later we would have found a way to gain full access to Kotacek's files without his knowing it. But it was not urgent, it could wait."

17

"And now?"

"His capture changes things considerably. We'd planned on going through his files when he died. He's an old man and a sick man. He has diabetes and a heart condition and is a cataleptic. He would probably have died within a year or two and that would have given us our opportunity. Now we can't wait—his death won't do us any good if he dies on the end of a rope in Prague. More important, we don't want the Russians to get to his files. I don't think he's given them anything yet. I don't think they know enough to ask for it. But during or after his trial, he may try to barter his information for his life. It would be a bad bargain for him. His files are worth a great deal more than his life.

"There's more to it than that. This doesn't entirely concern you, but I've never felt that it hurts an agent to know what the hell is going on and why. The Czechs are likely to make a big show out of his trial. They'll stir up a lot of anti-German feeling at a time when we don't want too much attention focused upon the policies of our friends in Bonn. Armament policies and such. There's more, but that's the essence of it. We want Kotacek out of Czechoslovakia. We want his files."

There was a long space of silence, with both of us trying not to carry the conversation any further. He finished his drink and I finished mine. He nodded toward the bottle, offering another, and I shook my head, declining. He lit a cigarette. I got to my feet, walked to the window, looked out. He took the bottle and filled his own glass. I turned, walked back to the couch, sat down.

Finally I said, "You want me to go into Czechoslovakia, get him out of jail, and sneak him out of the country."

"Yes."

"All by myself."

"That would probably be best."

"Why? Why not the CIA or someone with manpower?"

"The Boy Scouts," he said. "No, that's unjust of me. There are certain operations they handle rather well. But suppose the Agency did handle this one, Tanner. What would you have? You'd have an official agency of the United States Government rescuing a little tin Hitler from a country that has every right in the world, legal and moral, to try him and convict him and execute him. If the CIA tried it and blew it—and don't think they're not fully capable of doing just that now and then—well, you can imagine the public reaction. Even if they got him out, the story would probably leak. And if it didn't, if everything went off without a hitch, we'd still be on the outside as far as Kotacek's files are concerned. He'd no sooner turn them over to us than to the Russians. If we twisted his arm, the information would be close to useless; the men involved would go underground. You see what happens? If we lose, we lose big; if we win, we still lose. No, there's a better way."

He put out his cigarette. "Suppose the man who rescues Kotacek is not a CIA man at all. Suppose he's a member of, say, the Slovak Popular Party and a group of other nationalistic extremist movements. Suppose his presence would be interpreted as an obvious instance of a neo-fascist sympathizer selected by the network of international Naziism to spring Kotacek from the trap. Now do you see how neatly you fit in?"

"I'm hardly a Nazi. And the Slovak Popular Party isn't fascist. It's more a cultural organization for the preservation of the language than anything else."

"True. But a number of its members are Slovak fascists."

"That sort of charge can be leveled at any group."

"Precisely. That's exactly why you'll be able to operate effectively in this affair. You can enlist the aid of a variety of persons who would have no interest in helping the CIA or the United States government. You can approach Kotacek

19

as a fellow conspirator, an advocate of Slovakian autonomy and, by extension, a natural part of the new international Fourth Reich. He will trust you. He will give you access to his files, and he'll never know it when you bring their information back to us. If you bring it off, Tanner, you win all the way."

"And if I don't?"

His smile had an element of treachery to it. "If you lose," he said, "then what has happened? A fellow Nazi has tried to rescue Kotacek and has been caught in the attempt. Perhaps he tries to identify himself as a U.S. agent. If he does, the charge is laughed off. Perhaps he is imprisoned. Perhaps he is able to escape. Most likely, he is killed." He frowned. "Which would be a pity, but not a tragedy. I would lose a most useful agent, but the country would not get a black eye. Can you see how much better you fit the scheme than all of the Central Intelligence Agency?"

3

There is a special method to be followed in jumping from a moving train, or, presumably, from any other similarly mobile object. One jumps in the direction in which the train is moving, falls with the body bent forward and the legs already in motion, and lands running.

I was quite familiar with this method. I had read of it often enough in books and had seen professional stuntmen display it frequently on the motion picture screen. And so I stood poised on the trestle of the Prague-bound train, waiting for my faithful Nazi comrade to slow it to around a dozen miles an hour, and fully confident that I could dismount from my perch with the agility of John Wayne's double.

Brakes were applied and hissed in protest. The train slowed. I stepped to the edge of the trestle, crouched, hurled myself off into the night, and wondered, now that it was too late for wondering to do much good, why all those Hollywood stars used doubles. If it was so easy, as easy as falling off a train...

It wasn't so easy. The ground was there ahead of schedule, and my flailing feet hit it wrong, and my couchant body was improperly balanced, and there was a wide gulf, it seemed, between theory and practice. I stumbled, I bounced,

I sprawled. And lay there, quite motionless, while the train picked up speed and hurried on toward Prague.

The damage was not as great as it might have been. I had managed to shred one trouser leg and most of the knee it had contained. The other leg was doubled up awkwardly beneath me, not broken, not sprained, but not in entirely perfect order either. I had bruises on the palms of my hands, an aching shoulder that I seemed to have landed on, and a bump on my forehead about the size of a robin's egg. On the other hand, I did not have my suitcase, which I had left on the train, or my breath, which I had left somewhere between the trestle and the ground.

I got up tentatively and determined that nothing was broken. I tried walking and found that both legs hurt, but that the one which had been twisted in the fall was worse than the one that had been torn up. I limped around for a while. I was supposed to go to the town of Moll and tell Kurt Pisek that Heinz Neumann had sent me. No. I was supposed to go to the town of Neumann and tell Kurt Heinz that Pisek Moll . . . No.

I sat down. Everything went around for a few minutes. Before long they would be stopping the train at Tyn. More policemen would board it, and this time they would wait for the real Evan Tanner to stand up. They would spend perhaps half an hour searching the train before it became apparent to them that I had somehow left it. Then they would blow whistles and draw up plans and begin searching for me.

So there was not a great deal of time. But I could not start searching for Moll or Neumann or Pisek until I could clear my head enough to know which was which. I had to make use of what time I had.

I stretched out on my back, placed my arms at my sides, closed my eyes, and remained that way for twenty minutes.

I had not chosen the ostrich's method of hiding from

22

danger. The play was one I had borrowed from Yoga, a deep relaxation technique which helped replace sleep for me. I lay very still, contracting and elaborately relaxing each muscle group in turn, then doing what I could to turn off my mind, making it as blank as possible. About twenty minutes had passed when I yawned and stretched and sat up again. I couldn't be sure of the time—my watch was another casualty of the fall—but that particular regimen generally takes somewhere between eighteen and twenty-three minutes.

I felt much better. The pains were still there but they didn't get in my way as much. More important, my head was working again. I had to go to the town of Pisek, where a man named Kurt Neumann lived. I would tell Neumann that Heinz Moll had sent me. Pisek, if I remembered the map of Czechoslovakia correctly, was a few miles east of the Vltava and about twenty miles up the river from Tyn. I was probably about ten or twelve miles from Tyn myself.

The sky was overcast, with no stars to offer a clue to directions. I could follow the tracks of the train, but I knew too well where they would lead. They would take me straight into the railroad station at Tyn, and I knew the sort of welcome that awaited me there. And, once they knew I had left the train, it stood to reason that their initial search parties would work their way back along the train's roadbed.

The Vltava River flowed parallel to the railroad line and seemed a better idea. I made my way over the tracks and went and saw the river less than a hundred yards away. My leg bothered me, but I managed to work my way down the grassy slope to the riverbank below. Walking was easier on level ground. I limped, but the limp became progressively less pronounced the more I walked and was almost entirely gone after a mile or so.

A couple of miles further, the river was spanned by a bridge of stone reinforced with steel pilings. I crossed to

23

the west bank and headed north again. When the moon finally broke cloud cover it was easier for me to see where I was going. The river glistened in the moonlight.

I began whistling something, and it took me a few seconds to place the tune. It was the theme from Smetana's *Moldau,* another name for the river along whose western bank I walked. I whistled more of it, then stopped.

The irony delighted me. The *Moldau* theme was doubly appropriate, tying in not only with the river but with my mission itself. It had been borrowed from Smetana's work to serve in a song called "Hatikvah," and so I was limping through Czechoslovakia, on my way to enlist the help of a Sudeten Nazi in the rescue of a Slovakian Nazi, while whistling the national anthem of the state of Israel.

It must have been around three in the morning when I hit the outskirts of Pisek. I was cold, my legs had lost their enthusiasm for walking, and, more than anything else, I was hungry. I hadn't eaten anything since Vienna. Several times along the way I had passed farms and thought about stealing a few eggs or even making off with a whole chicken and roasting it hobo-style at the river's edge. But each time the risk had seemed disproportionately high.

Now, though, if there had been a plump hen handy, I might have eaten her, feathers and all.

The sky was still dark. It was a bad hour to call on strangers, whatever their politics. Etiquette aside, I had no way of locating Herr Neumann. Moll had not thought to give me Neumann's address, and some twenty thousand people live in Pisek. At a better hour I could scout around and ask directions, but not at three in the morning.

And there was another problem, not so demanding at the moment as hunger, but even more vital in the long run. As things stood, I would be about as inconspicuous in the streets of Pisek as a Negro on a snowpile. I was bruised and battered

24

and moderately dirty, and my clothes, American in cut, were at least as battered and a good deal dirtier than I. Once Pisek woke up and I entered its streets, I would not precisely blend with my surroundings.

I waited for the dawn in a small farmyard on the eastern edge of the city. The sky lightened, and I realized for the first time that the country was beautiful, lush and green, mostly flatland but rolling gently in spots. I saw lights go on in the farmhouse, and when I came closer I could hear movement within. There was no bell, so I knocked.

A man, short, thick-set, opened the door a crack and peered out at me. He asked me politely what I wanted.

"Food, if you have some to spare," I said. "I am hungry, and can pay. I have money."

"You do not live near here?"

"No."

"It is early to be traveling."

"I have just awakened. I slept in a field."

"In my field?"

"No. Across the road."

"I will be back in a moment."

He closed the door and I waited while he went to talk it over with his wife. I knew he wouldn't call the authorities— no phone wires ran to the house. He reappeared a few moments later and opened the door for me. I followed him to the kitchen and he pointed me to a seat at the round wooden table.

"Is ten koruna too much?"

"Not at all," I said. I found a pair of five-koruna notes in my wallet and gave them to him.

"If it is too much, tell me. I do not really know what to charge you. This is no restaurant, you know."

"It seems perfectly fair."

"Well," he said, and took the money. His wife turned from the stove and smiled tentatively at me. She brought

25

over a plateful of eggs and potato dumplings, all scrambled together.

"There is coffee," she said. "And I will bring you some rolls, and I will heat some sausages. Have you come from very far away?"

"From Ruzomberok."

"I do not know it. Is it far?"

"It is to the east, in Slovakia."

"Ahh, that is very far. And you have come all this way?"

"He is hungry, Frida," the man said. "Let him eat."

I was even hungrier than I had realized. The eggs were fresh and had been cooked to just the right turn, neither too wet nor too dry. They were seasoned nicely with paprika. The bits of potato dumplings were light and fluffy. The sausage, thick red-brown blood sausage, was delicious. The coffee was hot and strong, almost as strong as the Greeks and Yugoslavs drink it, but tempered with a healthy dose of sugar and fresh cream.

"You have hurt yourself," the man said. "Your leg and your hands. You will want to dress your wounds, perhaps to bathe. We have a tub with hot water; we got it just last year."

"The year before," Frida said.

"Whenever it was. And afterward my wife can patch your trousers. It is a bad rip there. You must have fallen down."

"Yes."

In the bathroom I cut all the labels out of my clothes, burned them, and flushed the ashes down the toilet. I took a hot bath and used some tape and gauze from the medicine chest to bandage my knee. The other bruises were just surface nicks and didn't need more than a good cleaning. The palms of my hands were already healing nicely.

I dried off, dressed, and rejoined my host. "These pants are too badly worn to repair," I said. "Perhaps you have an extra pair you could sell me?"

26

"I doubt that mine would fit you. But Frida can patch yours, and you may buy new clothing in town."

"Of course," I said.

"My son's clothes might fit you, but he is not here. He left last year. No, pardon me, it was the year before last. I remember that it was the same year that we got the hot water, and that was not last year, although I always think that it was. My son Karel is in Paris now. He works in a very fine restaurant there. He is only a busboy the last letter we had, but he has hopes of becoming a waiter. Is that where you are going? To Paris?"

"No, I am going to Pisek only. I—"

"Please." He looked away, as if embarrassed. "You have no luggage, not even a change of clothing, and yet you have enough money to pay ten koruna for breakfast without a second thought. You speak Czech very well, but with a slight accent which I cannot identify. But I do know that it is not a Slovak accent. A Slovak gives himself away because with certain words he uses the Slovak words or the Slovak pronunciation, and even here, this far in the west, I can identify a Slovak accent. And you are traveling to Pisek, presumably for a reason, but you do not know anyone in Pisek and must sleep in a field and come here for your breakfast."

"I guess I didn't fool you."

His eyes crinkled, amused. "Would you fool anyone? Your suit has been treated badly, but I do not believe it has been slept in. I would guess instead that you have been walking most of the night. The suit is a good one, too. You are a man of some substance, perhaps a professional man. If you do not wish to tell me, we will not talk anymore."

"No, I don't mind."

"Ah."

"I am from Poland. A town near Krakow."

"That would have been my guess, that or Hungary. Though the Hungarians generally go directly through Aus-

27

tria. We saw some Hungarians in 1956 but then there were so many of them that they went in all directions. You are not going west into Germany? That would be an even harder border to cross, if you wished to get into the Western Zone."

"I am going to Austria."

"Ah, that is a better idea. You will stay in Austria?"

"I don't know."

"That is your business, of course. And of course you would not want to tell anyone too much." The eyes showed that he was amused again. "I have thought of going, you know. But it is not that bad here, and every year it gets better. It is not Paradise, but when was this poor country ever Paradise? Before the war, well, the government was good, but one never knew how long it would be in power. And we were not nearly so prosperous." He shrugged. "One year the hot water, another year a milking machine, little by little things come to us. Some of the young people are impatient, like my Karel. But when one is old one learns patience, and that one place is rather like another. Still, your case is different, is it not? Your problem is political?"

"Yes, you could say so."

"You were a teacher in Krakow? Perhaps a professor?"

"You are very perceptive."

"Perhaps I should be a detective, eh? Sherlock Holmecek?" He laughed. "But I am glad we were able to talk, you and I," he said, suddenly serious again. "You will want peasant clothes, so that you will not stand out so against your surroundings. I have a few things of Karel's. He did not take them, and she does not wish to throw them out. You know women. She thinks he may some day return, and it costs nothing to humor her by keeping the clothes. Wait a moment."

He returned with a pair of heavy woolen pants and a rough gray work shirt. They were a little large on me, but not noticeably so. I dressed, and he inspected me from all

28

angles and decided that I looked the part better now. "A common laborer looking for work," he said. "But wait another moment," and he came back with a peaked cloth cap. I placed it on my head, he looked at it, adjusted the angle, and we agreed that the picture was now complete.

"A common Czech laborer," he said. "But I do not think you should say you are from Slovakia. Perhaps I am not the only Sherlock Holmecek in the country, eh? Tell them you are from—let me think—Mlada Boleslav. Yes. You lost your job in the brewery there and tried to find work in Prague, and there you were told that they needed workers at the Pisek Brewery. They do not, as it happens, which will save you the discomfort of actually being hired. I would personally suggest that you do all of your traveling in the daytime, but that is your business. To me, a man walking at night would be more suspicious. And you will put your wallet away, please. I told you that we are not in the restaurant business, and for that reason I intend to return your ten koruna. We are not in the secondhand clothing business either. I can take no payment."

"But I can pay—"

"Perhaps you can pay, but I cannot take the money. Believe me, you will need the money. Our money is not worth as much in the West. Karel told me his earnings and I could not believe it, and then he told me what he must pay for his room and I could not believe that, either." He shook his head. "You may find it is not as good there as you think. I hope not, I hope it is good for you, but you may be surprised."

He made me take back the ten koruna. At the door, his wife pressed a brown paper parcel into my hands. Sandwiches, she explained. I had liked the sausages so much ...

I ate the sandwiches on the road into Pisek. The breakfast had been a big one, but I was still hungry. I found a twenty-koruna note in with the sandwiches. I couldn't think of a way to return it to them, so I put it in my wallet.

A wonderful people, the Czechs, I thought. And I thought again, for perhaps the hundredth time, what a shame it would be to deprive them of the pleasure of hanging Janos Kotacek.

4

I didn't begin looking for Neumann at once. I walked into Pisek and asked first how to find the German neighborhood. The first clerk I approached became quite indignant, pointing out that the stigmata of national origin, like the false boundaries of class lines, had crumbled under socialism, and that thus such a concept as a "German" neighborhood was dialectically obsolescent. The next clerk I tried was less colorful but more helpful. He told me that most of the Germans in Pisek lived in the northeast corner of the city, and told me approximately what streets to take if I cared to walk there.

Whatever effect socialism may have upon the stigmata of national origin, Pisek very definitely had a German neighborhood. You could not mistake it. The signs of business establishments were all in that language, and nine out of ten street conversations were conducted in it. Here, I felt, they were more likely to know Neumann and less apt to become suspicious of anyone who came looking for him. I tried a grocer and a druggist with no luck. The butcher shop next door to the druggist proved more rewarding.

The butcher said, "Neumann? Neumann? Ah, little Kurt! Of course I know him, two blocks over, one block down, the gray house with the blue shutters. Number 74. But what would you want with little Kurt?"

He gave me no chance to answer the question. "Ahah! But your business is not with Kurt at all, is it?" He wiped his fat hands on his apron. "The daughter, eh? Oh, they come from far to see that one. And who can blame them?"

"Well, I . . . you know her?"

"Don't be shy. And who doesn't know Neumann's Greta? But a word to the wise—" He leaned forward, winked lewdly. "—You'd better spout off with the old Nazi line, you understand? The old Hitler bullshit. Instead of love and marriage whisper to her of purity of race and living space for the expanding German nation. The old Aryan routine. But take care that you only whisper or"—a throaty laugh— "or, by God you'll have the damned Czech police there in bed beside you!"

When I rang Neumann's bell I half expected the chimes to ring out the first four notes of "Deutschland Uber Alles." But there was only a flat buzzing sound, and then the door opened, seemingly of its own accord. I did not see the man who had opened it until he spoke. I had been looking over his head.

He was certainly no more than four and a half feet tall. His head was large, with straight black hair combed to the side in a partially successful attempt to hide a large bald spot. His complexion was dark, his teeth pointed and yellow.

"Herr Neumann?"

"*Ja?*"

"Heinz Moll told me to see you on a matter of the most urgent importance." I looked around furtively, a needless precaution, as I had already made reasonably certain that no one was following me. "May I come inside?"

He snapped erect and tried to click his heels together. The effect was lost. One of his thin legs was shorter than the other and ended in a clubfoot encased in a built-up shoe.

32

It did not lend itself to the military bearing he was trying to project.

"You will follow me," he said.

I followed him. The sitting room where he took me was clean and comfortable, furnished with an overstuffed sofa and matching chairs, a small upright piano, dark draperies, and a worn imitation Oriental rug. He motioned me to the couch, closed the drapes, and sat down in one of the chairs.

"I suppose you wish to get out of the country," he said. "You are too young to have served the Fuehrer, no? No matter. It is not easy to move a man out of Czechoslovakia. This filthy police state. Between the Slavs and the Jews, a decent German has little freedom these days. But it can be done, a man can be moved across any border. And, in the meantime, you will be safe here."

"I don't want to escape from Czechoslovakia."

"Oh? That is unusual."

"I am here illegally, with the police searching for me. My mission is here, in Czechoslovakia. In Prague."

"Most unusual."

"You know of Janos Kotacek?"

"The Slovak? The papers have been full of it. The fool returned here and was captured."

"He did not return. He was kidnapped in Portugal."

"The swine!"

"Yes. It is my task to rescue him from his captors."

"You alone?"

"Yes."

He nodded thoughtfully. "It is a noble task," he said. He got to his feet, took one of a pair of crossed dueling sabers from the wall over the piano. "Of course, Kotacek is a Slovak. A Slav. He is in no sense a German. But one cannot deny the work he has done for the cause."

"He is an important man."

"No doubt." Neumann slashed air with the sword. "It is

the mark of German maturity that we are able to make use of the best of the inferior races. Years ago I heard a speaker explain that the Slovaks might be considered the Slavic equivalent of the Germans. It was at a rally to develop support for the Slovak Republic. Such men can be very useful to us. And I don't have to tell you"—the sword sang viciously—"that after our ultimate victory, our allies among the inferior races will be suitably rewarded. Men like Kotacek will be sterilized, of course, but there will be no need for actual extermination. It is one thing to improve the racial characteristics of mankind. It is quite another to reward valuable service."

"Of course."

"Though there will be no need to sterilize Kotacek himself, I suppose. He must be very old."

"And an invalid."

"Ah. And it is very important for him to be rescued?"

"It is vital."

"Your name?"

"Tanner. Evan Tanner."

His brow furrowed. "That is an unusual name for a German. You are not a Slovak yourself, are you?"

"I am German. But I was born in America and have always lived there."

He nodded solemnly. "Then we can understand each other, you and I. To live in a foreign land and long for the glory of one's true home. We Sudeten Germans were forgotten for years until the Fuehrer spoke out for us. No doubt it is the same with our countrymen in America. Forced to live among inferiors, forced to see pure Aryan blood polluted by Jews and Slavs, separated unfairly from one's homeland."

He returned the saber to its place on the wall. "How is it for those of us in America?"

"Bad."

34

"Ah, but it is bad everywhere. I read an article in an American magazine once. I wonder if there was any truth in it?"

"What did it say?"

"That the Fuehrer is alive and living in Argentina. I suppose it is a lie, but one wonders."

"One may always hope."

He straightened up again. "You speak wise words. One can always hope. No man who has served as such an inspiration, as a force for the salvation of Germany, as a leader in the struggle for the development of a finer, purer race, no such man is ever truly dead." His right hand leaped up and out; his clubfoot snapped against his good foot. "Heil Hitler!"

I echoed his words.

For the next hour or so Neumann was drunk with enthusiasm. It was Nazi racial theories, even more than Pan-Germanism, which filled him with zeal. He talked about the Jewish menace and the manner in which Communism had evolved from the fusion of Slavic and Jewish racial weaknesses. He discussed the dangers of Chinese expansion and asked my opinion of a pamphlet he had read recently which suggested that the Chinese were descendants of the Ten Lost Tribes of Israel.

"There is food for thought there," he said. "One can readily detect the Jewish cleverness behind the mask of Oriental inscrutability. If the Japanese are the Germans of the Orient, then surely the Chinese are the Orient's Jews. Don't you agree, Herr Tanner?"

"It seems possible."

"Even the appearance has points of similarity. Not the skin color. That of course is deceptive. But consider a Chinese without his yellow skin tones. The sly eyes, the hooked nose—"

"Pardon me, but I don't think I've ever seen a Chinese with a hooked nose."

"I presume you've heard of plastic surgery?"

"Well—"

"Of course. Don't be naïve, Herr Tanner."

He plunged onward, but came up with nothing quite as provocative as the Jewish-Chinese theory. It *was* tempting, certainly. I couldn't quite see it as the basis of neo-Nazi philosophy, but surely something could be done with it. Perhaps an organization designed to promote the Jewish religion on the Chinese mainland. I'd have to see about it when I got back to New York.

"But I am talking too much," he said at last. He was not the first person in the room to have realized it. "There is work to be done. You need information, of course. You must know where Kotacek is being held, what is being done with him. I am very good at discovering things, Herr Tanner. I can move through the city and speak with the proper persons and learn a great deal." His lips curled in a sudden smile. "This may surprise you, but I have found that people do not fear me. They are not afraid of me and speak freely before me."

He took my arm. "I will show you to your room. It was my wife's room when she was alive. She died several years ago."

"I'm sorry."

"Thank you, but it was a blessing when she passed on. My Trudy was in poor health all her life. A weak constitution. She was never the same after Greta was born."

My room was large and light and airy, overlooking a small garden where flowers grew in properly disciplined rows. "Sleep if you are tired," Neumann said. "I will see Greta and tell her of your arrival. She is completely trustworthy. She shares our views."

"You must be proud of her."

"I am. It is such as she who will bear the *Ubermensch*—the Superman. But it is devilish hard to keep the Jews away from her. They lust after her. If those swine—" He shook his head violently. "I will send her home. She will cook for you. Perhaps she will go to Prague with you and help you with this Kotacek. Only see that the filthy old Slav keeps his hands off her. I beg that much of you!"

I had seen the father, and I had now learned that the mother had been sickly all her life. I thought of the butcher: *The daughter, eh? Oh, they come from far to see that one.* No doubt they did; she probably worked in a carnival sideshow.

I stretched out on the bed, picked up a pamphlet from the bedside table. It was in German. The title was *The Myth of the Six Million*, and it exposed Auschwitz as a legend created by the Jews of Moscow and Wall Street, acting in concert to defame the German people in the eyes of the world. There was an abundance of marginalia penned in by a tiny crabbed hand, and extensive passages were underlined in blue ink and further accented by marginal exclamation points. The pamphlet's thesis had three main points: that no Jews had been exterminated, that the number killed did not even begin to approach six million, and that next time the job would be done properly.

I read it and whistled the *Moldau*.

I had finished the pamphlet and was midway through a book called *Czechoslovakia: A Nation in Name Alone* when someone knocked at the door. I got off the bed and opened the door.

"Herr Tanner?"

"Yes?"

"I am Greta."

I found this quite impossible to believe. If that crippled dwarf had combined with a sickly little woman to produce

37

this blonde goddess, then all theories of heredity had been permanently repealed. She was tall, almost my height, and her long blonde hair melted over her shoulders. Her eyes were a deep, vivid blue. Her body was long and leggy and yet more than abundantly curved. An old Norseman would have carved her on the prow of his ship; whatever his skill, he could not possibly have improved on the original.

"You are staring at me."

"I am sorry."

"I am not. I do not mind." She licked her lips. "My father told me all about you. But he did not tell me you were young. I expected someone his age. I am not disappointed."

"Uh—"

"You must be hungry. Come downstairs. I will fix you some lunch and we will talk. My father said that you had many interesting things to say about the question of race. I would be interested to hear your views."

I followed her downstairs. Her bottom swayed leisurely from side to side as she walked. Her father had said that the Jews had lusted after her. I did not find this at all difficult to believe. I was suddenly certain that she was devoutly lusted after by Jews and Czechs and Slovaks and Germans and Russians and Hindi and Thais and Sumatrans. Anyone who saw her was likely to have the same reaction. It was not simply beauty, which, when all is said and done, may be a chilly asset. She had beauty in abundance, but she also had a special primitive quality that left one with no doubts concerning her obvious function in life.

She was not to talk with, she was not to cook, she was not to produce children. She was not to knit sweaters, to write plays, to dig ditches, to sing songs. She had been placed on earth for the singular purpose of lovemaking. That was what she was there for, that and nothing else.

"Some fried ham, Herr Tanner? And a stein of beer?"

"That would be fine, Fräulein Neumann."

"Oh, not so formal, please. Call me Greta."

"Greta."

"And I will call you what?"

"Evan."

"Evan. That is an unusual name, is it not? I do not think I have ever heard it before."

"It's not uncommon in America."

She brought the food and watched in silence while I ate. The ham was good, perhaps a little too salty but otherwise fine. The beer, according to the label, had been bottled right there in Pisek. It tasted very much like the Prague beer I had had now and then in New York. There is none better in the world.

When I finished she took my arm. "Now," she said, "we must talk. We will go to your room. It is quieter there."

We walked arm in arm up the stairs. Now and then her body brushed lightly but purposefully against me. My eyes kept stealing over to look into the front of her dress.

She was a Nazi, I told myself reasonably, and it was loathsome enough to rescue a Nazi, let alone make love to one. On top of that, she had a fiercely jealous father who was presently vital to the success of my rotten mission. And, if a third reason was needed, there was the fact that my mission to Prague was hazardous enough without the unnecessary complication of a romp in the hay with an Aryan maiden.

We entered my room, and she kicked the door neatly shut. She seated herself on my bed, and I looked around the room for a chair, and there wasn't one. I sat on the bed beside her. She yawned and stretched and sighed, and I tried to keep my eyes away from her chest with the approximate success of a moth trying to pay no attention to a flame.

"How old are you, Evan?"

"Thirty-four."

39

"Thirty-four! And I am only twenty-two. Do you realize what that means?"

"What?"

"You are old enough to be my"—she licked her lips—"my lover."

As soon as she left the room—assuming she ever did leave the room—I would have to take a cold shower. That was supposed to help. I wondered if they had a shower. I wondered if they had cold water. I wondered if it would really help.

"My father says that I will go to Prague with you, Evan."

"I don't think so."

"But of course I will!" She turned toward me, serious now, the gush of sex momentarily stanched. "You cannot go alone. Have you ever been to Prague? Do you know the city?"

"No, but—"

"I have been there. I know the town well. And I can help you. And you can trust me, and whom else can you trust in this country? My father could find friends of his, friends who might go with you, but I would not trust them. The government has spies everywhere, you know. Even in our own Bund there are undoubtedly spies. Why would you not want me to help?"

"It's a dangerous job for a woman."

"Is it less dangerous for a man?" She shook her head violently. "No, no, it is settled. We will go together. Papa will learn what there is to be learned, and we will make our plans, and we will leave for Prague tomorrow night after the meeting. Then—"

"What meeting?"

"Our local Bund. The Sudetendeutsche Bund of Pisek. After you address the meeting, we will—"

"After I what?"

"Address the meeting. It was Papa's idea."

40

"I just bet it was."

"Will you listen, please? The government police know you are in the country, right? But they do not know why. Tomorrow you will appear at the meeting. You will give them the usual inspiring speech about the need to annex the Sudetenland once again to the Fatherland. We have heard it often enough, but it is a message we never tire of listening to. There will be spies at the meeting, of course. Throughout the country there are spies. They will report you to the authorities, and the authorities will guess that you are traveling through Czechoslovakia trying to stir up German communities. They will not like this."

"Can you blame them?"

"You don't understand. They will know that you are in Czechoslovakia, but they will miss the point of your visit. Right now they suspect you are here to liberate a Slovak. This may make them unsure. They will still want to catch you, to arrest you, but perhaps they will be less certain that you will turn up in Prague. And, while they comb this area for you, you and I will go to Prague tomorrow night and make our plans to get the Slovak out of jail."

I didn't say anything. She watched me, her eyes anxious. There was a certain amount of lunacy in old Neumann's idea, but at the same time it might have a grain of merit to it as well. Any sort of false trail might make the game easier when we got to Prague.

"You will do it?"

A bloody Nazi speech to a batch of Sudetenland fanatics. How on earth could I manage to get the words out? I thought about this, and even as I did so I felt the old phrases coming automatically to mind. Just the same old pap they had been listening to for years, that was all it would have to be. And why shouldn't I be able to do it?

"All right," I said.

"Oh, good," she said, and she turned to look directly

41

into my eyes, and the ice-blue of her own eyes turned suddenly to the hot blue of a gas flame, and all at once she lunged at me and wrapped her arms around me and tumbled me down onto the bed. Her breasts pressed against my chest and her hips bounced merrily and her mouth was hungry.

She's a Nazi, I kept telling myself. Forget how her mouth tastes, forget how her body feels. Forget she's a woman. And forget that two and two is four, and that the sky is blue. And—

She drew slowly away from me. "There is no time now," she said. "No time at all."

I didn't say anything.

"My father will be home any moment now. He is always furious when he catches me with a man. Do you know what he does when he catches me?"

"What?"

"He whips me. Do you know where he whips me?" She picked up one of my hands and touched the appropriate parts of her body. "Here," she said, "and here, and once even here. Can you imagine?"

I couldn't stop imagining.

She arose reluctantly from the bed; she stepped languorously to the door of the room. "My father will not come to Prague with us," she said. "We will be alone."

I did not say anything.

"You'll take me to Prague with you, won't you? Even if I am a woman?"

"Yes."

"Perhaps *especially* because I am a woman?"

"Perhaps."

"Aryan men and women must labor together to rebuild the Fatherland," she said. It had the air of a memorized speech. Perhaps I would deliver it to the Bund the next night. "You're a nice Aryan man. And I'm an Aryan woman. I think we might enjoy . . . laboring together."

42

"It might not even seem like labor."

She giggled. The door opened, and she vanished, and the door closed behind her. I rolled over on the bed and told myself again that she was a Nazi. The thought did not seem to have retained its earlier impact. I tried to invent my speech for the Bund and had worlds of difficulty concentrating on it. I opened the windows and tried to air her scent from the room. It lingered persistently. She had not been wearing perfume; it was the sweet smell of Greta herself that clung to my bedspread.

I went into the bathroom and took a cold shower. It didn't do a damned bit of good.

5

"So it is settled," Neumann said at dinner. "You and Greta will go to Prague together."

"Yes."

"And you will speak tomorrow night at our meeting."

"Yes."

"I'm sure you will be an inspiration to our membership, Herr Tanner." He sighed. "You are an activist, you see. And what are we? Passive sympathizers, if the truth be known, and little more than that. We shout out 'Heil Hitler!' We pledge ourselves to the cause of *Anschluss* with Greater Germany. But what is it that we do? We do nothing."

"Papa, that's not true!"

He turned to her. "Oh? But it is true, my little one." His little one was a foot and a half taller than he was. "What do we do? We make speeches and listen to others make speeches. We read pamphlets and books. We contribute money when it is needed, but never give so much that we impoverish ourselves. And beneath it all we live our comfortable middle-class lives. We drink our beer and eat our schnitzels and sausages. We vow that we would die for Germany, but you see few of us dying. Lip service, that is all it is."

A word from me seemed called for. "People like you

and your daughter," I said, "are the backbone of our movement."

"You are good to say so."

"It is the truth."

"Perhaps. But how can we be at the backbone, we who have so little in the way of backbone ourselves?" He broke off sharply, pushed his chair back from the table, jumped to his feet. "It shall be different in the future," he pledged, his back as straight as possible, his chest out and his chin in. "Heil Hitler!"

He strutted away from the table like a toy soldier. Greta put her hand on my arm. "Sometimes Papa takes things too seriously," she said. "He cannot relax. He feels he has been given a mission to perform for Germany, but he does not know what it is, and it eats at him and drives him mad with frustration."

"He should know that he is doing his part."

"Perhaps he wants to do more than his part. He did not show this to you, but he is very proud that Heinz Moll sent you to him, that he is able to be of assistance to you. It is important to him. He has encountered, oh, a great deal of trouble over the years, you know. Not only since the war. Even during it, when we were a part of Germany. I was not even born then, but I have heard talk. It was very hard for him."

"How?"

She hesitated, then licked her lips. "He might not forgive me for telling you."

"I'll say nothing to him."

"Please don't. You see, Papa was a member of the Sudeten Nazi League even before the annexation. Long before the annexation. And they teased him then. His theories about race."

"Why?"

"His ... well, his physique. He is short, you know. And

46

he is dark, both his hair and his complexion. And his eyes, I don't know if you noticed, but his eyes are brown."

"Not exactly the Nordic ideal."

"No, not at all. And his foot, you know. Poor Papa." She lowered her eyes. "Mama told me it was even worse for him during the war. You know of Hitler's policies for improving the race? People who were found to be...uh...defective—"

"I know."

"I would never question the wisdom of the Fuehrer's ideas. I believe in them very strongly myself. But they cannot be applied to everyone. Not to the leading supporters of the Fatherland."

"There are exceptions to every rule," I said.

"Exactly. In any case, certain persons had to be eliminated. Incorrigible criminals, lunatics, giants, cripples, dwarfs." She shuddered violently. "Papa was almost classed as a dwarf. Can you imagine? He is short, but you couldn't call him abnormally short, and certainly not a dwarf. But they judged solely by height. Fortunately he wore a pair of special shoes for the examination, and the doctor—he was an old Party friend—listed his height at 4' 7". They were transporting those under 4'6". So he passed. But you can imagine his humiliation."

I nodded.

"And then his foot, his poor foot. It was a birth defect, not a genetic trouble at all, but some fool of an administrator determined that Papa ought to be sterilized for the good of the race. It makes me sick to think of it. Fortunately he managed to perform an important personal favor for a Party official and the orders for his sterilization were destroyed." She lowered her eyes again. "He was frightened when I was born. I was born during the last months of the war, though he did not know then that it was that close to ending. He did not believe Germany could be beaten. He did not realize

47

that the Jews would manage to stab us in the back just as they did in 1918, and that we would be beaten by their betrayal. And he was desperately afraid that I might . . . that I might resemble him. That I might be very short, and dark, and perhaps even lame—"

"I'd guess he has nothing to worry about."

"No." She smiled and brightened the room. "It is fortunate, isn't it? That I turned out as I did?"

"Very fortunate."

"He feels I am living proof of his pure Aryan heritage. He says that he is of a special class of German, like Goebbels. A short German who grew dark. But pure Aryan nevertheless."

"It is the obvious answer."

"I'm glad you understand."

Later I sat in the living room with Neumann. Greta was upstairs. "One favor I have to ask of you," he said.

"Ask it."

"You must be very careful of Greta."

"I don't understand."

He turned aside, sucked pensively on his colorful teeth. "This Kotacek, what do we know of him? He works for the Reich, true. But he is a Slovak, also true. And blood will tell."

"You are concerned that he—"

"Yes." His eyes probed mine. "She is only a child, Tanner. Only a child. And you know what old men are like when lush young girls are near. A good German has strength of character, he is able to resist temptation. But this Kotacek. Now I would say nothing against him, you understand. I do not know the man. Still . . ."

"Of course."

"You will make sure that no harm comes to her?"

"Yes."

48

And a few minutes later, when Greta joined us, he went over what he had learned in the streets. "The trial will begin in four days. That gives you time if you act swiftly. Janos Kotacek is being held in Hradccy Castle. Do you know it?"

"No."

"An old castle of the days of the Bohemian nobility. When our forces marched into Prague, the castle became Hradecy Prison. Czech saboteurs were interned there, along with racial undesirables awaiting shipment to the Fatherland." Neumann paled slightly, then regained his coloring. "After the war the Communist government converted the structure into a castle once again. They thought it might serve as a tourist attraction. It is an inspiring building on the riverbank, with big towers and gables and the like. Would you like to see such a building?"

"Certainly."

"Would you travel thousands of miles to Prague just for the pleasure of examining such a building?"

"Probably not."

"Neither did anyone else. And, as this government remained in power, it discovered it had more need for a prison than a dubious tourist attraction. So the castle was converted a third time, made once again into a prison. From what I have heard, Kotacek is being held in one of the high towers. There is a guard at his door, and there are guards throughout the prison."

"I see."

"It may be difficult for you, but you will have Greta's help. And of course a pair of Germans can outwit a clutch of stupid Czech guards. Besides, you will have two or three days to do it."

"Can we get help in Prague?"

"Help? I don't understand."

"From other loyal Party members."

He shook his head. "I know many such men in Prague.

49

But I know none I could trust absolutely."

"But the two of us against a fortress—"

"I am sure you can manage it."

I thought for a moment. I closed my eyes and pictured the two of us, Greta and I, tripping blithely up the prison, she bumping her fine body against me every step of the way, while the Czech guards showed us on our way, up to Kotacek's tower cell and down again.

I said, "Perhaps it might be worth the risk if we could just enlist half a dozen men."

"The risk is too great. I could not permit it."

"If you picked the men you were most sure of. Or if you let me sound them out myself—"

He was shaking his head. Then, with great reluctance, he said, "Perhaps I can tell you something that will show you just how great the risk is. You can see this house, that it is a nice home? And that we live comfortably, Greta and I?"

"Yes."

"Have you thought to wonder what it is that I do for a living?"

"It's not my business."

"Of course it is your business."

Greta said, "Papa—"

"No, it is right that Herr Tanner should know. I do not work. I am paid by the filthy Communist government to inform them of the activities of the Bund. Of course I tell them nothing important. I fill their ears for them, I give them trivia and withhold more valuable information. But now do you begin to understand? Even I am a spy for them, even Kurt Neumann, and I am the only man in Czechoslovakia you can trust!"

We left our planning Operation Kotacek about then. Greta brought cold beer and we knocked off a few bottles each and discussed the divine mission of the German people. The

50

mood grew mellow. Neumann broke out a bottle of slivovitz, assuring me that they didn't make as good a plum brandy in Germany as they did in Prague. He poured healthy slugs for each of us and we put a good dent in the bottle. Greta kicked off her shoes and sat down at the piano, and she played the "Horst Wessel Lied" and some other old-time favorites.

I entered into the spirit of things and sang most of the score of Weill and Brecht's *Die Dreigroschenoper*. They had never heard it before. I explained that the Fuehrer had had a museum set up in one room of which *The Threepenny Opera* was played twenty-four hours a day, day in and day out.

"No wonder it sounds so good to me," Greta said. "It must have been his favorite music."

I left that one alone. I hadn't bothered to explain that the music was played at what Hitler had called the Museum of Decadent Culture. That particular room was very popular for a time; it was supposed to be the only place in Nazi Germany where you could hear anything but Wagner.

"The melodies are so fresh, so alive!"

"And the words have a harsh German bite to them. Good Berlin realism. Not polluted by Jewish Communism."

I decided that Brecht in particular would be enchanted by the scene. And through it all, through the beer and the singing and most of the bottle of slivovitz, Greta flirted more and more openly. She brushed against me when she went for more beer. She leaned far forward to refill my glass and to assure me in the process that there was nothing beneath her blouse but Greta. She's a Nazi, I told myself for the thousandth time, and it did about as much good as the cold shower.

The night was threatening to last forever. Finally Neumann glanced at his watch, hauled himself to his feet, and announced that it was time for bed. "Herr Tanner must be

51

tired," he said. "And tomorrow will be a busy day for us all."

I wished them both a good night and went upstairs.

I used to tell people the whole thing, about not sleeping, the wound in Korea, the effect it has had on my life, the medical opinions I've received, everything. I learned before very long that this was a mistake. All I ever accomplished was the dubious pleasure of having the same conversation five or six times a day, with no particularly interesting variations. *Will it shorten your life? Yes, probably, but let's talk about something else, shall we? What do you do with all your time? Read, write letters, work, play baseball, learn languages, dally with girls. Don't you get tired? Of course I do, you idiot. Did you ever think of going on television, something like "To Tell The Truth" or "I've Got A Secret?" No. Never.*

So I didn't bother adding the interesting fact of permanent insomnia to the Neumann storehouse of interesting facts about Evan Michael Tanner. Instead I went upstairs to my room, closed the door, and stretched out on the bed to finish *Czechoslovakia: A Nation in Name Alone*. I couldn't keep my mind on what I was reading but I went through the book anyway and finished it in about half an hour. It was the usual sort of diatribe, but I came out of it with three or four good points for my speech to the Bund.

I closed the book, got out my clothes, turned down the bed, flicked off the light, and stretched out on my back. My eyes were tired and my leg had begun to bother me again. I closed my eyes to concentrate on empty black space and saw nothing but Greta, eyes half-lidded, body bare, mouth delicately obscene. I tried blinking the image away. There are several good Yoga techniques for blanking the mind, and I tried all of them, and none of them worked.

So I went through the various muscle groups, relaxing them in turn, and I was not particularly astonished to find

52

that there was one particular muscle group which stubbornly refused to relax, an island of unrelieved tension in a sea of tranquility.

Until finally the doorknob turned and the door eased soundlessly open and she entered my room. I could not see her in the darkness but I knew it was her. The smell of her filled the room.

I didn't move. She padded softly across the room and stood for some silent moments by the side of the bed.

"Evan? Are you asleep?"

I did not say anything.

"I couldn't sleep, Evan. I tried, but I just couldn't. Are you asleep, Evan? I think I know a way to wake you—"

She lifted the bed sheet, drew it down. Her hand, soft, cool, trailed down over my chest.

"Oh!" she said, delighted. "You're not asleep at all, are you? You were only pretending!"

And she rolled her fine Aryan body on top of me.

I touched her and kissed her. She panted and squirmed and giggled. I thought of the cold shower I had taken earlier; I might as well have tried to put out a forest fire with a cup of water. *She's a Nazi*, an inner voice cried, albeit weakly. *Politics make strange bedfellows*, a stronger voice retorted. And that particular dialogue ended, and another wordless dialogue took over.

She had switched on the bedside lamp. I was lying back with my head pillowed on the sweet warmth of her thighs. Her golden hair hung down free, framing her breasts and brushing my face. Her hands, which had raced so trippingly over the keyboard to play the "Horst Wessel Lied," now raced just as trippingly over me.

"It's asleep now," she said.

"I'm not asleep."

"Not you. It."

53

"Oh."

"It was awake when I came in, and I have put it to sleep. Will it sleep for very long?"

"Not at this rate."

"Good. You know, I expected it the minute I saw you. That's why I was so excited."

"Expected what?"

"That you were Jewish."

"What?"

"Oh, don't worry," she said. She giggled. "I won't tell anyone, Evan. Because then I would have to tell Papa how it is that I know, and he would be very angry. He would whip me. Here, and here, and—"

"Yes, I know. I'm not Jewish."

"But of course you are."

"No, I'm not."

"But"—her fingers moved—"this is the proof, is it not? Jews are fixed this way and Germans are not. A rabbi does it, no? I always wondered what he did with it afterward."

"In America," I said, "that particular—uh—operation is performed on almost everyone. In the hospital. By a doctor."

"You are joking with me."

"I'm not joking."

"You are telling the truth?"

"Yes."

"And this is done to everyone in America?"

"Almost everyone, nowadays."

"By a doctor?"

"Yes."

"Do they have to use a Jewish doctor?"

"Any doctor can do it. Greta—"

"And you're really not Jewish?"

"Really. Greta—"

"Oh."

54

"Is something wrong?"

"No, I guess not. But I was certain that you were a Jew. I thought so from the beginning, and then when you told me your name—Evan—I thought it was like Ivan and that you were a Russian Jew. Why are you laughing?"

"I'm sorry."

"And then now, after we did it, I was sure of it. I never enjoy it that much except with Jews."

"You..."

She shrugged. "My father would kill me."

"He probably would."

"I knew he would. I share his feelings on race completely, Evan. You must believe that I do. But in the dark, and lying down, it is a different matter. I don't know why. It just happens that way."

None of this is really happening, I told myself reasonably. I suffered a concussion when I leaped from the train, and I have been dreaming all of this. The girl and her father do not exist. None of this exists. It is all a dream, caused by a devastating blow on the head. In time it will all pass away.

"Evan? Do you think I am terrible?"

"No."

"I can't help myself, really. And I don't think they should be exterminated. I think that is a bad idea, extermination. What is the point of it?"

"The purity of the race—"

"Ah, but I have an answer for that!" Her eyes lit up. "Not extermination but sterilization. Do you see? And then a girl like myself could have Jewish lovers whenever she wanted and be very very happy all of the time and never have to worry about becoming pregnant. The race would not be polluted with Jewish blood, and yet I could have my pleasure, and... You are laughing at me, Evan."

"I'm laughing at everything."

55

"You will not tell my father?"

"Of course not."

She changed position, stretched out beside me. "You're very nice," she said. She kissed me, and her soft hand resumed its dalliance. "I think it is a marvelous idea, that everyone should have this operation. It must have been a Jewish trick, but I think nevertheless that it is a good practice. So naked it is, and so defenseless."

"Unprotected."

"Yes."

"But dangerous when cornered."

"Ahh!"

"Do you realize what would happen if your father were here?"

"Oh, but he's sleeping. He will not—"

"But if he did."

"Oh—"

"He would whip you."

"He would, yes, he would."

"He would whip you here—"

"Yes."

"—and here—"

"Yes, oh, yes—"

"And even here—"

"Ahhhh—"

6

When she finally left I went through the deep relaxation ritual again, this time with considerably more success. After twenty minutes of it I got dressed and went downstairs. I found a handful of books that looked interesting, including one in Czech; I could speak the language well enough but hadn't read it intensively in some time, and wanted to brush up on it before we went to Prague.

There was an old atlas, too, and I carted it upstairs with the rest. Assuming that we managed to liberate Kotacek, we still had the problem of getting him out of the country and back to Lisbon. The short way would take us through either Germany or Austria, through the Iron Curtain and into the sunshine. That was the fastest way, but the more I thought about it the less I liked it. Those were the borders the Czechs would guard at once. They would seal them up tight, and slipping Kotacek through would be just slightly more difficult than threading a needle with a camel.

Even if we took advantage of the element of surprise and rushed past the German border, we wouldn't be ahead of the game by any means. He'd be as hot in East Germany as in Czechoslovakia, and, as a war criminal, wouldn't exactly get a hero's welcome in West Germany either. And

I didn't even want to think about the problem of getting him across the West German border. Or, God forbid, of chucking him over the Berlin Wall.

The plan, then, would be to work our weary way south and east. There were little pockets of Slovak autonomists who would hide us in the first dark days after the rescue. South of Slovakia, in Hungary, there were political extremists of various persuasions upon whom I could call in an emergency. Most of them would cheerfully slit Kotacek's throat if they knew who he was, but I could coach him to play whatever part the circumstances demanded.

From Hungary we could go to Yugoslavia, in many ways my favorite country. I was sure I could establish an underground railroad that would carry us all the way to the Greek border with a minimum of effort. And Greece was no particular problem. There were Macedonians in the northern hills, anarchists and such around Athens, even a Stuart legitimist on the island of Corfu.

From Athens, a plane to Lisbon. And in Lisbon I could work some devious miracle, get access to Kotacek's records, and abandon him to his past and future sins.

It was comforting to plan the escape route. In outline form, it appeared easier than I expected it to be in actual practice. Moreover, by concentrating on the escape I could postpone thinking about the rescue itself. Janos Kotacek was in a castle tower in Prague, and my Nazi nymphomaniac would be my sole assistant in getting him out, and the less I thought about that, the better I felt.

I opened the atlas, hoping to trace a tentative exit route on the map. I located a double-page map of Europe and looked for Pisek, and then for Prague, and then stopped, and squinted in puzzlement, because there was no Czechoslovakia on the silly map. There was just one big Germany, spreading from France to Russia, and . . .

Of course. The damned atlas had been printed in Frankfurt, in 1941. And Europe had looked rather different at that date, especially when sighted from that particular point of view.

It was pointless to look for escape routes. Out of curiosity I thumbed through the atlas and checked out other continents, other countries. Africa was carved up among Britain and Spain and France; Ghana was still the Gold Coast; the Congo still belonged to Belgium; and Liberia was the only independent country on the continent. The map of Asia showed such items of nostalgia as French Indo-China, British India, Portuguese Goa, and Tibet. No Laos, no Cambodia, no Vietnam. No Pakistan. Large slabs of China and Korea were shown as Japanese possessions. Manchuria was labeled Manchukuo.

Rather far-reaching changes in only twenty-five years. I wondered what new changes would come in the next quarter-century—which countries would be larger and which ones would shrink or disappear, which new countries would emerge, which old ones would cease to exist. Perhaps there would be an autonomous Slovakia by then. Perhaps the Irish would win over the six Northern Counties, perhaps a Stuart would sit on the throne of England and a Bonaparte on the throne of France.

Perhaps Macedonia would be free, and Armenia, and Croatia, and Kurdistan, and all those other pockets of patriotism that clamored for freedom. Perhaps all the lost causes to which I wholeheartedly subscribe would find fulfillment. It seemed impossible, but the old atlas proved that the impossible had a disconcerting habit of happening in spite of all rules of logic.

I closed the book. It hadn't helped much, but it had done wonders for my state of mind.

The day went quickly. I breakfasted with Neumann and Greta. I won three games of chess from him, and he left the house for a few hours, and Greta and I went to my room. I told her I would have to save my strength for our work in Prague, but she found a way to change my mind.

She was gone all afternoon, perhaps searching for a Jewish lover, and I spent the time reading, loafing, soaking in a hot tub. We had venison steaks for dinner; a friend of Kurt's had shot a deer in one of the government forests, and Kurt had bought three filets to celebrate my speech to the Bund.

"We must celebrate in advance," he said, "because you and Greta will want to leave immediately after."

We walked to the Bund meeting around seven-thirty. It was held in the basement of a Lutheran church about half a mile from the Neumann house. We slipped in through a back entrance, marched single file down a long darkened flight of stairs, and emerged in a room full of old Germans.

It was a shock. I had expected a beer hall full of bristling young Storm Troopers, and instead I found myself in what looked like an old folks' home in Yorkville. The median age was somewhere between fifty-five and sixty. Around seventy-five men and women sat in straight-backed chairs and talked companionably to one another in German, pausing now and then to refill their glasses from the beer keg at the rear of the room. They reminded me, more than anything else, of the American Communist Party—a handful of old fossils living on dreams of past glory, and about as much of a revolutionary force as a librarians' conference in Emporia.

"Evan? You seem surprised."

"It is nothing, Herr Neumann."

"Perhaps you expected more younger members? Not at the Bund, I am sorry to say. Of course we have the German Youth League for our schoolchildren. They go hiking and camping and win prizes for physical fitness. No Hitler Youth by any means, but we do what we can."

I took a seat near the back of the room, with Greta on

one side and her father on the other. We were close to the beer keg, which was fortunate, because the first hour of the meeting was intolerable. There was an insufficiently brief speech of welcome by the chairman, a reading of the minutes of the previous meeting, a secretary's report on correspondence with other Bunds, a treasurer's report on the state of the organization's finances and the lethargy of some members in paying their annual dues, and, finally, a long address by a doddering white-haired gentleman on the current state of the German business community in Mexico City. Some relative had written him an overlong letter on the subject, and the old fool stood up there and read it to us, inserting his own parenthetical remarks from time to time.

Throughout all of this ritual, the audience paid only cursory attention to what was going on in the front of the room. Everyone was drinking and nearly everyone was chatting, with individuals pausing from time to time to assure themselves that the meeting was still officially in progress. At first it was comforting to note that Nazism wasn't quite the menace nowadays the *Police Gazette* might give one to understand, but as the evening wore on I began to grow annoyed at the towering wave of apathy which flowed over everyone in the room. If they were going to be Nazis, I thought, they at least ought to work at it.

When the old white-haired man finally reached the end of his letter he smiled apologetically and sat down to the same smattering of polite applause that had greeted everything, even the statement that the Bund was several thousand koruna in the red. I was irritated. There ought to be a way to reach these people, to get them moving one way or another. They were, after all, political extremists. Revolutionaries, if you will. They were not supposed to act and react like a Rotary Club.

"And now," the chairman was saying, "I have the honor to introduce a distinguished Party member from America

61

who has come all this way to talk to us about the greater ramifications of the problems of Germans in Czechoslovakia. Herr Evan Tanner."

Inevitable polite applause.

I walked down the aisle, took my place at the podium. I had my speech all planned, an innocuous ten-minute affair lauding the contributions of Germans to the culture of the world and of Sudeten Germans to the growth of Germany, lamenting the poor state of Germans in Czechoslovakia, and calling for unification of East and West Germany with the nation enlarged to include German areas of Czechoslovakia. The usual pap, and I'm sure it would have gone over well enough, drawing occasional moments of attentiveness from segments of my audience and ending, predictably enough, in a round of polite applause.

But something happened.

"Brothers, sisters, fellow Germans—"

The proper opening. But I paused then, and held the pause, and the conversations died down and eyes were drawn to me. My heels clicked, my arm shot up and out, and my voice rang out: "Heil Hitler!"

The response was about fifteen seconds delayed. They were out of practice, but they had been properly conditioned and I had rung the right bell; they had to salivate. The roar came back—Heil Hitler!—not as loud as it might have been, not raising the rafters, but loud enough and firm enough to get the ball rolling.

"I look around," I shouted, "and what do I see? I see Germans. I see Germans living in a strange land. I see Germans ground into the dust by the heel of a foreign oppressor. And who is the oppressor? The Czech! Who is behind the Czech? The Russian! And what villain pulls the Russian's strings? *The Jew!*"

More eyes were on me. I realized suddenly that no one had gone for beer since I began to speak. Either the keg had gone suddenly dry or I was actually beginning to reach these people.

"Germany has been torn in half," I cried. "She lies bleeding from a wound that leaves her in pieces, one half a pawn for the Jews of Wall Street, the other a police state under the thumb of the godless Hebrew Bolshevists of Moscow. And Berlin, the grandest city in the world, is an island in a turbulent sea with the indignity of a wall down its spine. And what of Austria? A German country ripped away from Germany, as the rest of the world tries to undo one of the Fuehrer's greatest accomplishments. Do you know what they say throughout the world? Do you know what they say? They say that Germany is dead!"

I dropped my voice to a murmur. "Is Germany dead?"

They expected me to answer it myself. I didn't. I let the question hang in the air, and finally a few adventurous souls said, "No."

"Is Germany dead?"

"No!"

"I ask you, is the Fatherland dead?"

A roar this time: *"No."*

"No?" I held out my hands, palms open. I turned my head slowly and gazed at every member of my audience in turn. "No? If Germany lives, if the Fatherland still breathes, you could not prove it by the state of our countrymen in this land they call Czechoslovakia. For everywhere I go I see our people downtrodden. Everywhere I go I see their children taught to speak Czech, taught by a government of Jews and Communists to forget their nation, to repudiate their name, to reject the fact that they are Germans. Are you Germans?"

"Yes!"

I shudder to remember the rest. There was a great deal more of it, all equally inane, as I and my audience moved inexorably to a fever pitch. Men were on their feet now,

63

shouting the appropriate responses. One old woman grabbed at her chest and pitched over on her face. A heart attack, probably. No one went to her rescue. They were too caught up in my words. They hadn't had a night like this since the Russian tanks freed Prague.

And I knew I should stop, knew that the situation was rapidly getting out of hand. A quick shift in tone, an inspirational ending, an appeal for funds or something of the sort, would have let me end it on a lower note. I knew this was the way to do it, but I had hold of something and couldn't let it go. I was a conductor and they were the orchestra, and the score called for crescendo straight through to the coda, and that was what they were going to get.

I cursed the Czech merchants who were sucking the life-blood of the German populace. I cursed the Czech officials who were raping German culture. I called for vengeance, and I told them that they would have to take vengeance themselves, and all at once I was demanding action now, not in the hereafter, not sometime in the future, but now.

"Out! Out! Out into the streets, out to meet the enemy! Meet him with fists, meet him with rocks, meet him with crowbars! Smash his windows and burn his houses! Out into the streets!"

And out they went. In a swarming furious mob, some hobbling on canes, some limping with arthritis, some blinking idiotically through bifocals. An old man broke up a card chair and brandished one of its legs as a club. A pair of women forced the door of the German Youth League's storeroom and passed out baseball bats and hockey sticks and Indian clubs. Off they went, into the streets, out to meet the enemy.

I ran up the stairs after them. On both sides of the street old men and women were heaving rocks and smashing windows. To my left two men had a Czech policeman by the arms while a woman beat him over the head with a chair leg. Further down the block a house was in flames.

Madness reigned. There were police sirens in the distance. Greta ran to me, threw her arms around my neck, kissed me. Kurt was pumping my hand furiously. "You are a hero," he shouted. "You have forged us into an army. Pisek will remember this day."

"So will I."

"But you must go now, you and Greta. And hurry! You have business in Prague. Hurry!"

"How?"

"Just run! The police will be here any moment. You cannot be caught; your work is too important. Both of you, run!"

We ran. We ran blindly, through the mob, away from the mob, down one street, around a corner, down another street. A third of the way down the block the sidewalk was thronged with a wedding procession. Men and women lined churchsteps, heaving things at a Czech bridal couple. A squat car waited for them at the curb, its engine running, a sign on the trunk lid announcing that they were newlyweds.

The groom, beaming foolishly, held the door for his bride. Greta snatched the girl by the arms, yanked her back, and pitched her into the crowd. The groom gaped. I hit him on the side of the chin, tucked Greta into the car, raced around it, hopped behind the wheel, and we were off.

7

We had about a block's head start on the wedding party. They were an astonished lot, and we might have been around a corner and out of sight before they thought to give chase had the car only cooperated. But it was sluggish and unresponsive, and by the time we reached the corner they were racing down the center of the streets after us.

I took the corner without reducing speed. The little car's rear end swung out like a jackknifing trailer, and we very nearly flipped over at the improbable speed of thirty-five miles an hour. Greta clutched my arm in panic. I used the other arm to keep us from knocking down a presumably innocent bystander. The wedding mob turned the corner, panting hot on our trail, shouting unintelligible things after us. The next intersection was blocked by two police cars, evidently en route to quell the Nazi disturbance. One of the police vans had nosed into the tail of the other, and the two drivers, resplendent in identical uniforms, were having a fist fight beside their crippled vessels.

I leaped the curb, swung around the wreck, and pressed onward. The car began to build up a little in the way of speed, and then the engine coughed and sputtered and stalled, and the mob was gaining on us.

The streets were lined with Czechs who had come out

to watch the fun. The police wreck was spectacle enough, but now they had the thrill of watching a wild-eyed mob run down a bridal couple. The vanguard of the mob had very nearly reached us when I made the engine catch again, and we were off in a cloud of monoxide.

"Where are we going?" Greta wanted to know.

"Prague."

"Oh, good."

"Which way is Prague?"

"North."

"Which way is north?"

"I don't know. On the map, it's straight up."

The damn car stalled again. The mob had very nearly disappeared from view and I thought they might have given up, but now that we had stalled they summoned up their second wind. I saw a pack of older teen-agers giggling at us from the curb. I got out of the car, tore the "Just Married" sign from the trunk lid, sailed it across the street. One of the kids asked me where I was going. I asked him how to get to Prague, and he gave me rough directions, and I talked with him some more. The mob was getting close.

"Hurry!"

I motioned Greta to be quiet, then spoke some more with the Czech boy. He wished me good luck. I got behind the wheel, closed the door. The mob was closing in again. Their ranks had thinned perceptibly, but we were still greatly outnumbered and our bargaining position looked weak.

"Can't you get this started?"

"I'm trying to," I told her.

"They'll get us. Why did you have to talk to that boy?"

"He told me how to get to Prague. Don't worry."

"But they'll catch us—"

"No, they won't."

The engine caught. I pulled away, less in a hurry now, and the mob came on strong, and the teen-ager's companions

68

moved into the middle of the street in a phalanx. Greta was staring out the window, taking it all in.

"They're fighting," she said.

"Yes."

"It's a brawl. They are all fighting, the wedding mob and those boys. Why?"

"To give us a chance to get out of here."

"But why?"

"I told that fellow you were going to be married off to an old man, a wealthy Communist bureaucrat. That you and I were in love, but your parents forced you into this marriage. And that I came out of the west like Lochinvar to rescue you." I turned the corner, taking it at a restful pace this time. "Juvenile delinquents are incurably romantic. It's that way the whole world over. They are helping the earnest young man save the beautiful young lady from a fate worse than death. They are fighting for youth and love and truth and beauty."

"It is good that they did not know who we are."

"Yes."

"They aren't following us anymore. I can't see anyone behind us. Is it far to Prague?"

"Don't you know?"

"I think it is about one hundred kilometers, but that is not what I meant. How long will it take us to get there?"

"About two hours. I don't know the roads, of course."

"Of course." She gave up gazing through the rear window, swung around and sat down beside me. "I have nothing to wear. Nothing but these clothes."

"There may be something in the trunk."

"You mean of the ones who got married? Her things would not fit me, I don't think. She was shorter than me, and thin. And quite flatchested."

"I didn't notice."

"I thought men always notice."

69

"Not always."

"The boy was your height. His clothes might fit you, though he too was very thin. Not at all handsome, either. He had no chin."

"Well, he has less chin now. That's where I hit him. Was he circumcised?"

"Now how do I know? I only—oh, you are making a joke with me, aren't you?"

"Yes."

"Where will we stay in Prague? Can we go to one of the better hotels? I have always wanted to stay in a truly beautiful hotel."

"We can't go to a hotel."

"Oh, because we would be detected. I understand." She was silent for a moment. "Then where will we stay?"

"I don't know."

"Oh. Will we have to be in Prague very long?"

"I have no idea."

"How do you think we shall rescue Herr Kotacek? Do you have a plan?"

"No."

"No plan at all?"

"No."

"We will just go there and try to figure out a plan, and then go ahead and do it?"

"That's the general idea, yes."

"I'm sorry. Would you like me to be quiet now?"

"I'd love that."

"I'm sorry. I will be quiet."

"Good."

She was remarkably true to her word. I had managed to find the main road to Prague, a two-lane affair that was reasonably straight and quite free of traffic. I stayed on it for about three-quarters of an hour and got most of the way to Prague, then got nervous about the road and took a turn to the left. I had the feeling that they might have guessed that Evan Tanner and the mad auto thief were one and the same, and that our road might have a welcoming party in waiting at its northern end. We drove west for a while, then found another road going north and worked our way into Prague from the northwest. No one took any particular notice of us.

The car worried me. No one had noticed it yet, and it was even possible that the license number had not yet been widely broadcast. Between the confusion of the Nazi melee and the milder but equally confusing rumble between the wedding guests and the teen-agers, the police might well have had their hands full. But my morning the Prague police would be looking for our license number, and by morning it would be light enough for them to see it.

I was reluctant to abandon it. It might come in handy later on, after we either managed to get Kotacek or failed in the attempt. Either way we would want to leave Prague in a hurry, and I didn't want to count on stumbling across a car with key in ignition and motor running a second time. But keeping it was risky, and even abandoning it could be risky; it would be a very obvious indication to whoever found the car that I was in Prague. They would probably guess as much by themselves, but why draw them pictures?

I stopped the car around the corner from a government petrol station, one of the rare ones that stayed open all night. Greta got out, and together we unloaded a pair of cheap new suitcases from the trunk. I raised the hood and performed some minor surgery on the engine—a wire here, a thing or two there. I got back in the car and tried the ignition, and nothing happened.

"Hell," I said.

"Was something wrong with the car?"

"Something is now."

71

I fiddled around, put back the loose wire, and tried the car again. It started this time, but the engine made a beautifully horrible noise. It sounded as though the whole thing would go up in smoke any minute. I left Greta on the curb with the luggage and drove around the block and into the petrol station. The engine clanked furiously. I cut it, coasted to a stop. The attendant came on the run. It sounded, he told me, like a meat grinder. I asked him if he could fix it. That, he said, was plainly impossible until morning, when the mechanic would be on duty. For his part, he sold petrol and oil, nothing else. But, I said, I had to drive to Pilsen for several days, and had to be there by morning. What could be done? Nothing, he replied. Could I leave the car, take a bus to Pilsen, and pick it up repaired upon my return? I could leave it, he assured me, but he could not guarantee it would be repaired when I returned. Such things took time. On occasion they had to send a long distance for a part. But the work, he went on, would be as good as any obtainable anywhere. . . .

He raised the garage door for me and I put the car to bed. If we needed it, it would be there. If not, it would still be there. And, in any case, it would be where no one would report it as an abandoned vehicle, and where no passing cop would take any special notice of its license number.

I collected Greta where I had left her. "I was afraid you would not come back," she said. "What happened to the car?"

"I left it to be repaired. Let's go."

"Where?"

"I'd like to have a look at that castle."

"At this hour? We should find a place to sleep. I'm exhausted."

"You have to sleep now?"

"Darling, it is the middle of the night."

"Oh."

72

"The morning will be time enough to look at the castle."

"I'm too keyed up to sleep, Greta. I want to see where they're holding Kotacek. I want to—"

"I know a way to help you relax."

"No, not now." I thought for a moment. "But you need a place to sleep, and we can't use a hotel. Do you have friends in Prague?"

"Yes, a few."

"Can you trust them?"

"No."

It was a bad country for trusting one's friends, it seemed. I closed my eyes and thought about Prague. There were various political friends of mine, but none of them struck me as ideal hosts for a young Nazi maiden. Then I remembered Klaus Silber.

"There is a man we can stay with," I said. "A man here in Prague, a friend of mine. He will give you a bed for the night, and then I will join you in the morning."

"Won't you sleep?"

"Perhaps I'll return in time to sleep a few hours. It doesn't matter."

"Will this man help us?"

"No. He is not sympathetic to our cause."

"Then why go to him?"

"Because he will pay no attention to us," I said. "He is a scientist, and a great one. An astronomer."

"A professor?"

"They do not allow him to teach anymore."

"Ah, I see. For political reasons?"

"No, he is not a political man. He will probably not want to talk with you at all. If he does, you might pretend to have difficulty with his language. No, that won't do. He must speak a dozen languages. Let me think . . ."

"Is something wrong with this man?"

"No, not really. He was in a concentration camp during

73

the war. It changed his view of the world. He's a Jew, so it might be better if he didn't know you were a German. What other languages do you have?"

"Just German and Czech."

"Oh. Well, be a German then, if he asks, but don't hand him any Nazi doctrine."

"I am not a fool, darling."

"I know. If he says anything that strikes you as strange, just pretend to agree with him. Tell him you are traveling with Evan Tanner, that I am on dangerous business. Tell him they are after us."

"Who is 'they?'"

"He will not ask. That will be explanation enough for him. Tell him that I am very much taken with his moebius-strip theory and feel it might offer an acceptable rebuttal to the Blankenstein Proposition. Can you remember that?"

"If I could understand it . . ."

"You can't, I don't think. A moebius strip is a band with a twist in it, so that it only has one side. Can you follow that much?"

"No."

"Good. Just memorize what you are supposed to tell him. Can you get it straight? *Evan Tanner is very much taken with your moebius-strip theory and—*"

She was a reasonably fast study. Once she had her lines down pat I tucked her into a cab and gave the driver Klaus Silber's address. I put the luggage in the cab with her and watched her disappear into the night.

Hradecy Castle was not terribly hard to find. I could have taken a cab there, but I didn't want anyone wondering why a man would want to look at a castle-turned-prison-turned-castle-turned-prison in the middle of the night, so instead I went looking for the place myself. I took a taxi to a hotel in Wenceslas Square and had little trouble finding the Vltava from there. I had a fair idea which direction would lead me to the castle. I headed in that direction, and there it was.

Even at that hour the structure was impressive. A broad base, about the size of a downtown bank. Long narrow windows trimmed with rococo gingerbread. Sixty feet up, the squarish base of the building gave way to a central peaked cathedral apex, with four rectangular towers at the corners. The towers extended perhaps another sixty feet or more, with narrow slits for windows. I could imagine how they were constructed on the inside. A taut spiral staircase running up each tower to the tiny roomlet at the top.

The defensive value of the design was obvious enough. Men posted in the tower rooms could remain quite safe while guarding the castle from all directions. Even a traitor within the gates would be hard put to knock out the marksmen in the towers. The spiral staircases were easily defended.

The towers made good dungeons, too. In one of them, I thought, Janos Kotacek awaited his trial and execution. There would be a guard posted at his door at the top of the long staircase. Perhaps there would be another guard halfway down the stairs. Perhaps not. But there would surely be a guard or two at the foot of the staircase, just as there were guards in the castle courtyard and in front of the castle gates.

Even if one got over the fence that surrounded the castle grounds, even if one managed the impossible feat of getting inside the castle walls, the whole business was still unworkable. It would be impossible to get up the staircase, impossible to get into Kotacek's cell, and profoundly impossible, once in, to get oneself and Kotacek out of there. The only possible exit would involve the removal of a couple of iron bars and a plunge of some hundred fifty feet into the waters of the Vltava River.

All out of the question.

I shouldn't have come in the first place, I told myself. I should have told the soft pudgy madman from Washington to go to hell for himself. I was not one of his boys. Just because I had used him once to get the CIA off my back, just because he had been gull enough to believe I was one of his agents, the man was handing me idiot assignments. And I, idiot, was taking them. Go to Prague. Storm a castle. Save a Nazi. Come home and await further instructions.

Bah.

Well, it simply could not be done. I would have to find some way to get out of the country and back to the States. Perhaps it would be worthwhile to stay a week or so with Greta and Klaus Silber until the government had a chance to forget me. Then out of the country, without Kotacek but with my head still fastened to my shoulders, and back to New York. Then, if my puffy little chief ever condescended to contact me ("Don't ever try to get in touch with us, Tanner. We'll always be the ones to make contact") I could tell him the job went sour. Or that it was easy, but I blew it—that might be best, because it would put him off the idea of using me in the future.

I felt a good deal better having decided all this. With all that taken care of, I slipped across the road and moved alongside the castle gate for a better look at things. Was the gate electrified? I studied it and couldn't tell. I squatted down a foot from it and looked through it at the guards. There were three of them in the front yard of the castle, one on each side of the massive door, one at the head of the walk. The two on the door were talking, but I couldn't catch any of the words.

Assuming one was fool enough to try, I thought, one would have to find some way to get the guards out of the castle. It wouldn't be possible to get past them, and without an army it wouldn't be feasible to take the citadel by storm. There would have to be some way to goad them all out and

76

deal with them one by one, and all without arousing suspicion from any quarter.

Nonsense.

I moved back from the fence, slipped around the side toward the river. There was a light burning in the turret at the left rear corner of the castle. Kotacek's light? Impossible to tell. Imagine negotiating each of those spiral staircases in turn, hunting for the right one. Climbing all the way up, then begging pardon when one stumbles on some arsonist or murderer, then heading down again and pressing on once more in the search for the Slovak Nazi.

Assuming that the fence wasn't electrified, I thought, it wouldn't be all that hard to get over it. Even limited to a two-person job, it could be scaled without all that much trouble. How high was it? Ten feet? Spikes on the top, of course, but toss a pillow over them and they'd be less of a problem. Or get a hacksaw and go through the spikes—no, not likely, not as thick as they were and not with the little time available. Still, a person *could* climb over. . . .

Nonsense. I wasn't going to try anything quite so harebrained.

Still, it was worth pondering, if only as an intellectual puzzle. Suppose one could get over the gate satisfactorily. Then what? Create a diversion at the rear of the castle grounds, draw the guards that way? No, small chance of that working. They wouldn't all rush out. A few would hang back, and they'd be doubly on their guard.

I looked at the river. Approach on a raft? Scale the walls with grappling hooks, something of the sort? I became dizzy at the thought. Even if it were possible—and I was quite confident that it was not—that would leave us up there in Kotacek's cell with no particular way to get out. And if we tried to carry the old invalid down the ropes to the raft— no, no, it wasn't even worth thinking about.

How could one draw out the guards? Start a fire in the

77

castle? Set off an air-raid siren? They'd probably take shelter right there. But some ploy of that sort had to be the answer. The best method would have to be one that avoided the scaling of walls and the climbing of fences. Some special stratagem that would permit us to walk through the front gates and up into the castle and into Kotacek's tower and out again.

It would have to be done at night, obviously. The castle had not entirely been made into a prison. The towers each contained a cell, but the two main floors seemed to have been converted into administrative offices of one sort or another, probably housing some special police branch. In the daytime, there would be more than a handful of guards to worry about. But at night there were only the guards.

How many of them? The three I saw, and, unless I was mistaken, at least half a dozen more on the inside. I drew back from the gate, followed it back to the front of the castle, then went on across the street. I worked my way around to the other side of the castle and kept my eye on the guards. It wasn't hard to see that they approached their tasks with rather less in the way of enthusiasm than, say, the Beefeaters at the Tower of London. I did not much blame them. It was late, the night was dark, no one was watching them (at least as far as they knew), and their job was the unromantic one of making sure that a sickly old Slovak didn't break out of his maximum-security cell.

They did about as well as could be expected. They did not stand firmly at attention, but neither did they slouch. They did not leave their posts, and yet they were willing to take a few steps one way or the other. They were not boisterous, but neither were they silent. I could hear them more clearly now, the two who stood at either side of the door. They were talking about girls, one boasting slightly, the other pretending disbelief in order to be told more details.

78

"Oh, come now," the second was saying. "Do you expect me to believe *that?*"

"You doubt that there are such girls?"

"I am sure you exaggerate."

"This one could have taken on an army," said the first. "At least a battalion, and quite likely a regiment. She could not get enough. You should have been there, Erno. She had more than enough to go around...."

They might almost have been talking about my little Greta.

I moved closer to hear them better. All right, I thought. So there was a way to do it after all. A long shot, but the whole business had been a ridiculous long shot from the beginning. All right, old mystery man from Washington, we'll take a crack at it. We'll bring your Nazi home for you. With all the trouble getting into the country and all the probable trouble getting out of it, it only made sense to do the job while I was there.

And now I felt quite noble and heroic, like Bogart and Claude Rains at the end of *Casablanca*. Very what the hell, it's not our war and we don't much care, but while we're here we'll give the Nazi a little bit of hell.

It's always pleasant to identify with Bogart. *Play it again, Sam,* I would say, and the rickety old piano would swing with the *Moldau* theme. *Play it, Sam,* I would drawl, and Greta Neumann would tickle the ivories with the "Horst Wessel Lied" and "Mack the Knife." *Play it again, Sam....*

I didn't even hear them come up behind me. No one stepped on a twig. There was just the tiniest intake of breath, barely noticeable, and then something got me behind the right ear, and the lights went out.

8

The first thing I noticed was that my head ached. I wanted to touch the sore spot, see if the blow had left a bump, and at that point I discovered that my hands were tied. I was sitting in a chair, and my hands were lashed together behind my back. I still hadn't opened my eyes. I wasn't entirely sure I wanted to.

This was trouble. The charges—inciting to riot, auto theft, God knew what else—would be enough to keep me many years in prison. The fact that I had been trying to spring Kotacek would add another thousand years to my sentence. And there was no one to call on for help. Not the U.S. government. Not the man who had sent me to Prague; he wouldn't lift a finger for me, and I didn't even know how to get in touch with him anyway.

My head hurt. There were voices around me, but I did not bother listening to them. I was completely dissociated. Coming to after having been knocked out is not much different from waking up in the morning, but I hadn't done the latter in better than sixteen years. I wasn't used to being unconscious, and I didn't like it.

Humphrey Bogart. Hah. I no longer felt like him at all. He would be on his feet now, I thought, bandying words nimbly with his captors, still cocksure and glib. I was simply not in his league.

". . . advance information," someone said. "He couldn't have been alone. We may be in for trouble."

"You should never have hit him."

"But he obviously knew about us. And would have given the alarm."

"I'm not sure of that."

"Any identification on him?"

"Just this damned French passport, but I don't think it's his. Fabre, it says his name is. But look at that picture. Doesn't look a bit like him."

"They all look alike."

"Don't be ridiculous."

"Why was he there if not to spy on us?"

"Who knows? Maybe he's a peeping Tom."

"And gets his thrills peeking at guards?"

"Stranger things have happened."

"Nonsense!"

I opened one eye cautiously. Something was very odd about the conversation, I knew, but I could not quite manage to dope out what it was. I scanned my surroundings. I seemed to be in a basement, rather dark, with one light bulb hanging from a cord in the middle of the room. There were four young men in civilian clothing talking beneath the light bulb. They had dark complexions and glossy black hair.

"The question, Ari, is what is to be done with him."

"We can leave him here."

"And have a man standing guard over him constantly? That won't do."

"Of course not. I did not propose it."

"Just leave him here, then?"

"Tied properly, hands and feet bound—"

"And return from time to time to feed him, perhaps?"

"It is only humane."

"I suggest we kill him."

82

"You, Zvi, have rather an appetite for killing, do you not? Just last month—"

"That is not true!"

"No?"

"Certainly not. One must not kill for the sake of killing. Neither may one avoid killing when it is the most expedient course available. You know that, and—"

"But we do not know who this man is!"

"Does it matter? He is dangerous."

"How do you *know* he is dangerous?"

"Does one wait until a snake bites before assuming that snakes are capable of biting? The man is a hazard to us."

"Not here. Not tied like this."

The argument continued. It would not be accurate to say that I lost interest in it. I was the man they were discussing. In tones of pure reason they were earnestly debating whether or not to kill me. No one is sufficiently blasé to be bored by such a discussion. But there was something about the discussion, something important, and I couldn't quite put my finger on it.

"Why not talk to him?"

"And believe his lies? Pointless."

"He might be a valuable captive. We could barter him."

"For the other? Not a chance."

"For our freedom, if we're caught."

"Why should we be caught? I suggest we put the matter to a vote."

"And I am frankly surprised, after the results of the last nationwide elections, that you still show any faith in the democratic process."

"There is a difference between democracy in microcosm and in macrocosm. Still..."

Oh, of course. I must had been addled by the blow on the head, I thought. I was listening to everything they said, and understanding everything they said, and able to know

83

that there was something about it all that was important, and yet I missed the most obvious thing of all. I didn't miss it exactly. I bypassed it.

They were all speaking Hebrew.

When you speak enough languages, and know them thoroughly, fluently, it is not necessary to stop and think just what it is you are speaking or listening to. You do not translate it mentally. You hear it and understand it and reply in kind.

Still, I really ought to have known at once that they were speaking Hebrew. I was in Prague. I could expect to hear Czech, or Slovak, or perhaps German. Not Hebrew. So the blow on the head must have had a rather extreme effect.

I opened my eyes. "He is awake," one of them said.

"Wide, awake," I said in Hebrew. "But my head hurts. What fool struck me?"

"He speaks Hebrew!"

"Of course I do. Where are we? What is this place?"

They gathered round me. "It may be a trick," one said. "I do not understand this."

"Will one of you please untie me?"

One moved closer, drew a knife. "We have made a mistake," he told me. "We took you for a government agent. I will cut you loose."

"Be careful, Ari!"

"Of what?"

"It may be a trick."

"You're a fool. The man speaks Hebrew."

"Hell! Eichmann spoke Hebrew."

"This man is a Jew."

"And do you suddenly trust all Jews, Ari? Do you think they have no Jewish agents? And no agents who speak our tongue?"

Ari put his knife away.

84

I sighed. Softly I said, "In the name of the All-present who brought Israel out of the house of bondage in Egypt, I swear not to rest until the Nation is resurrected as a free and sovereign State within its historic boundaries, from Dan to Beersheba on both sides of the Jordan. To obey blindly my superior officers; not to reveal anything entrusted to me, neither under threats nor bodily torture; and that I shall bear my sufferings in silence. If I forget thee, oh Jerusalem, let my right hand forget its cunning. . . ."

I went through to the end of the oath. I watched their faces, first suspicious, then open in disbelief, then slack.

It had been a guess, and their faces said it was a good one. They were Israelis, of course. Their conversation, what I'd caught of it, didn't sound like that of government agents. They sounded more like a special breed—mavericks, terrorists.

Just before the Second World War a group of radicals split the Jewish army, the Haganah, to form the more militant Irgun. And later, after that war and another one, extremists split the Irgun in turn, refused to accept the partition of Palestine, and called for the expansion of Israel's boundaries to the traditional proportions—from Dan to Beersheba on both sides of the Jordan. The group had dwindled in size over the years. Its members had been called many things, from the only true patriots and the spiritual descendants of the Maccabees to fanatics and Jewish fascists.

Their official name was the Stern Gang. I had been given their oath six years ago in a two-room walk-up apartment on Attorney Street in a Puerto Rican neighborhood on the Lower East Side. I had repeated the words with one hand on a Bible and the other on a gun. Over the years I'd had little contact with the organization. Once I sheltered a Sternist fund raiser who had come to New York without a passport. On several occasions I sent money to an address in Tel Aviv. Now and then a bulletin came in the mail—a report of a successful punitive expedition against a Syrian or Jordanian border post, a lament over the results of a Knesset election, a protest over the continued existence of various war criminals. The Stern Gang was not the most active organization which could count me as a member, but it had long been one of my favorites.

Zvi said, "Your name?"

"Evan Michael Tanner."

"English?"

"American."

"The oath you just repeated..."

I told him where I had received it, and when, and from whom. The name was one they recognized. They devised a few more verbal tests and I passed them. The one called Ari took out his knife again and cut me loose, and I got to my feet and rubbed the circulation back into my hands.

"What can we get you, brother?"

"An aspirin would help."

"An aspirin—oh, your head. I'm afraid we have no aspirin. Haim, do you have aspirin?"

"No, I don't. Would sinus pills help?"

I touched the spot on my head. It was not badly swollen, but still ached. "I don't think so."

"I'm sorry we had to hit you."

"It's all right." I glanced around. "Where are we, anyway?"

"A block from the castle. The house is empty. We have blocked off the basement windows so the light cannot be seen."

"Are there more of you?"

"Just we four. And you? Did you come alone?"

"Yes."

"From whom did you receive your orders?"

"I did not come under orders. It was my own idea."

"To get the Butcher of Slovakia?"

86

"Yes."

"What made you come?"

"I had family," I said, "in Bratislava. Kotacek shipped them west. To Belsen." I thought for a moment, looking for the right phrases. "I hoped to kill him myself, if I could. Or to see him hanged, at the least."

"A great undertaking for one man."

"Perhaps. And you? You came to take him to Israel for trial?"

Zvi's eyes flashed. "We know better, thank you. Those fools in Tel Aviv would only succeed in making a hero out of him. They very nearly achieved that with Eichmann, you know. By the time he dangled from the rope half the world had summoned up pity for the devil. Kotacek will die in Prague."

"He will have a trial," Haim said.

"But I suspect he will be found guilty," said the fourth, whose name I had not yet caught. "With we four as the jury—"

"We five," Haim said.

"We five. With we five to judge him, it is to be expected that he will be found guilty. We have brought a rope."

"Ah."

"With which we will hang him. And then we will return to Israel, and it will be announced that the Stern Gang has tried and executed the Butcher of Slovakia. Of course we will deny it officially, but the world knows what to believe."

"How did you plan to get to him?"

They looked at each other, then at me. "That is a difficult question," Ari said. "Gershon here"—now I knew all their names—"thinks it can be done by force. Storm the castle, shoot the guards, grab Kotacek and get off with him."

"The guards are slow," Gershon said. "It would take them ten minutes to draw their revolvers. By that time—"

"We stand a better chance at the trial," Ari insisted.

87

"They would not allow us in the courtroom."

"But there is certain to be a way. He will be conducted from his cell to the courtroom and back again at the end of the day. We would seize him en route. And think of the dramatic effect!"

"But it would be too difficult."

"And storming the castle would be easy?"

I said, "There's another way."

They looked at me.

"It would involve another person, a girl. She is not a member of our organization"

"Who is she?"

"Actually, she is not even Jewish."

"Oh?"

"As a matter of fact," I said, "she is German."

"And you would use her in our plans? You must be mad." This from Zvi.

"She could be very useful. I had planned to use her myself in this manner, but it might be very difficult—the plan calls for more than two. With six of us it would work very neatly."

"And not with five?"

"With five, yes. Without the girl, no. She is essential."

"You trust her?"

"Completely."

"Why should a German girl help us?"

"She has deep sympathies for the Jewish people," I said. "She saw *Anne Frank* and was deeply moved. The spirit of the Jewish race has probed the depths of her being and touched far within her." That last, I thought, was at least true. "Believe me, she will help us."

"What is her name?"

"Greta Neumann."

"She will do what you tell her?"

"Yes."

"And how would this plan of yours work?"

88

"We would take the Slovak from the castle," I said. "Without firing a shot. We would go in after him and take him out and no one would be the wiser."

"Do you know how well the place is guarded?"

"I just know of the three guards outside. How many others are there?"

"In the daytime," Haim said, "dozens. At night, considerably fewer. The three which you saw, and one on post outside Kotacek's cell, and two at the foot of the staircase. If only we could get Kotacek to cooperate, there is one plan we might try. You know how sick he is. Everything in the world is wrong with him. Diabetes, his heart, catalepsy—whatever that is.

Catalepsy is a form of epilepsy, except the victim doesn't thrash around during a seizure. He lies like a corpse, and usually wears a little silver tag around his neck begging undertakers not to embalm him by mistake.

"Everything wrong with him," Haim went on. "So if he could pretend to be sick, and then one of us went into the castle carrying the little black bag of a doctor—"

"I don't think it would work," I said.

"No, we have abandoned it." He shrugged. "If your plan is workable, we ought to hear it. What is it?"

I told them.

"I don't know," Zvi said. "It sounds . . . I don't know. Do you really think it could be done?"

"Yes."

"And the girl?"

"She is perfect for the part. You will be convinced when you meet her, but for now you may take my word for it. She is ideal."

"And she would do it?"

"She will cooperate in every sense of the word."

"She is here in Prague?"

"Yes, at a friend's house."

89

"You can bring her here?"

"She will be here tomorrow night. We can put the plan into operation immediately."

"Let's go over it again," Gershon said. "I would like to hear it one more time."

We went over it several more times. I wanted to get an idea of the position of our quarters in relation to the castle, so Ari took me upstairs to the attic. He carried a flashlight with a very thin beam. We climbed the stairs in silence, moved to the attic window. From there we had a perfect view of the front of the castle.

"When we planned to take the castle with a direct assault," he said, "we thought of posting one man here with a rifle. But there are so few of us, that would leave just three to storm the place. It is a good view, is it not?"

It was an excellent view. He handed me a pair of binoculars and indicated Kotacek's cell, in the left rear tower. From our angle I could see the light in his cell window but nothing more.

"We'd better go now, Evan. We all need sleep. There is an extra bed on the first floor, if you need it."

"I slept most of the day. I'm not tired."

"You'll be leaving, then?"

"I could stand guard, if you'd like. I want to go for the girl, but I can't get her until morning."

"We usually stand guard in two-hour shifts."

"I could take the whole night, as long as there's something to read."

"You wouldn't fall asleep?"

"No. I'm not at all tired."

We went downstairs, and they discussed it. They decided that they were all very tired and would be delighted if I would stand guard and let them sleep uninterrupted. I was

90

glad of this, not because of any mad passion for guard duty but because I read their decision as a sign of trust. It was vital that they trust me. Otherwise I would have a devil of a time in betraying them.

They all slept in the basement, on mattresses which they had lugged down from various second-floor bedrooms. The house evidently belonged to some important Communist Party functionary who had been sent somewhere as ambassador. I sat in the same chair I'd been tied up in, facing the cellar stairs and reading with the aid of the pencil-beam flashlight. The basement windows had been so well masked off that I couldn't even tell when dawn broke. My companions awoke one by one, and we had breakfast together, and then I left to collect Greta. It was midmorning by the time I reached Klaus Silber's bungalow.

He let me in, wreathed in smiles. "So we finally meet, Mr. Tanner. I have so greatly enjoyed your articles and letters. And there is much that I would wish to discuss with you."

I wanted to talk at length but had no time to spare. Still, I let him persuade me to have a cup of tea and some rolls. We had a good talk. I asked about Greta, and he told me that she was fine. "But nervous, Tanner. A nervous girl."

"She's been sick."

"Ah."

I went upstairs and collected Greta. "You should have told me the man was insane," she said. "I was afraid you would not come back for me. Such a man to leave me with!"

"He's a fine old gentleman."

"He's out of his mind."

We returned downstairs after I'd had a look through the two suitcases from the bridal couple's car. Greta had been right about the bride's clothes. They were too small for her, and not especially attractive anyway. "You'll go shopping

91

today," I said. "I want you to buy the most exciting dress you can find. Cut very low in front, and tight, and provocative."

"Then you ought to take me to Paris."

"Can't you find anything in Prague?"

"I will see. Why? What is this all about?"

"I'll tell you later."

I found that I could squeeze into the groom's clothes, but most of them did not seem worth the bother. I put on fresh socks and underwear but kept my own shirt and pants and sweater and cap. We closed the suitcases and left them in the closet.

As we left, Klaus shook hands warmly with each of us in turn. "Be very careful," he said. And, smiling, "Don't fall off!"

We left the house. Greta said, "Do you know what he meant by that? 'Don't fall off'?"

"Yes."

"He meant don't fall off the end of the world."

"I know."

"He believes the world is flat. Like a great big pancake, he said, only he said that the pancake was too simple, that it was more complicated but that I probably could not grasp it. Do you know what he was talking about?"

"Yes."

"He thinks the earth is flat. He says he is a member of something, and that you are, too. I forget the name."

"The Flat Earth Society."

"Yes. Are you?"

"Yes."

I finally persuaded her to change the subject. I told her I had been to the castle, and that I had figured out a way to rescue Kotacek. "It may be very difficult," I said. "I met some men who will help us. They are Israelis. Zionists."

She gasped. "They will kill us!"

92

"No, they'll help us."

"But—"

"It's very complicated," I said. "You'll have to play a very important role in the proceedings. It may be dangerous."

"No danger is too great for the glory of the Fatherland."

We stopped at a café, ordered cups of coffee with cream. I went over the plan with her from beginning to end. Her eyes flashed as she took it all in. Twice she started to giggle.

"It is a wonderful plan, darling."

"Do you think you can do your part?"

"Yes. I like my part. Tell me. These four boys—what are their names again?"

"Ari and Gershon and Haim and Zvi."

"Such beautiful names. Like music, do you know? What do they think I am? A Jew?"

"No. A sympathizer."

"Ah. What are they like? Are they handsome?"

I described them. Her eyes went that gas-flame blue again. "I should like to meet them now," she said.

"Later. First we'll have to buy a dress for you, something to fit the part."

"And then I'll meet your Stern Gang friends?"

"Yes."

"I can hardly wait."

9

The fence was not electrified. Gershon had determined as much that afternoon by giving a young boy a few copper coins to run up and touch it. The urchin raced to the fence while Gershon stood watching him, waiting to see if the lad would be electrocuted. He touched the fence, turned, waved to us, and darted away. Gershon was not entirely satisfied; he thought it likely that they might turn on the electricity only at night. So before we went over the fence he padded up to it carrying a gray and white alley cat in a sack. He unbagged the cat and tossed it gently at the fence. The cat bounced off, miaowed, looked hatefully at us, and took off hell for leather in the opposite direction.

So much for that. Haim had brought a stepladder from our basement. He set it up alongside the fence. Greta, her pure Nordic beauty resplendent in the sexiest dress available in Prague, kissed each of us in turn. One by one we ascended the ladder, cleared the ominous spikes, and dropped more or less soundlessly to the ground below. When the five of us had made the trip, Greta folded the ladder and carried it off out of sight.

We waited silent in the darkness. I crawled toward the front of the castle to keep an eye on things. After an eternity, I heard the tapping of Greta's new high heels on the sidewalk. She walked to the entrance at the front gate. She spoke with the lead guard and told him what she wanted. He said something, she said something, she leaned forward, his eyes crawled down the front of her dress, and he spun around and walked back quickly to confer with his two comrades at the castle door. The three of them whispered furiously to one another.

The lead guard returned to Greta. She pressed up against him, kissed him. He looked around vacantly, and Greta took her arm and pointed to where the five of us lay in waiting. He patted her bottom. She giggled appreciatively.

"I won't be long," he assured the other guards.

"That's your problem," one answered him, and the other laughed.

They approached us, walking quickly and purposefully across the thick carpet of grass. Twice the buffoon stopped to take her in his arms and kiss her. "Hurry," she panted gloriously. "I can't wait."

They reached us. She turned her back to him, and he unhooked her dress. She stepped out of it. "Now take off your clothes, my darling," she suggested.

He peeled off his uniform in great haste. They embraced, kissed. "Ah, heaven," the guard said, and Zvi dented his skull with a length of lead pipe. The naked Czech collapsed in Greta's arms. She drew reluctantly away from him and he slipped gently to the ground.

"You might have let him finish," she whispered.

"No time," I whispered back.

She shrugged philosophically, and her bare breasts bobbed in disappointment. Ari stripped off his clothes in the darkness and put on the uniform which the guard had so considerately taken off. It was a good touch, that; it saved us the trouble of undressing an unconscious man, which as every drunkard's wife will attest, is no mean task. Zvi and I tied up the guard, bound hands and feet, fastened gag in mouth.

96

Ari looked good in uniform. He was an inch or two shorter than the guard, but that was minor. He skirted the castle door as widely as possible, took up his position near the front gates, and talked to the other guards over his shoulder, to keep his face as well hidden as possible.

We had taught him two Czech expressions, and he delivered the first one now. "She's waiting for you."

And the inevitable question, "How was she?"

And Ari's second Czech phrase, one not to be found in the Berlitz guide book. "Best piece of ass I ever had!"

The guard at the left of the door came next. He first looked around comically, as if to make sure that Big Brother was not watching. Then he set his rifle on the doorstep and slipped around the side of the building to where Greta was waiting. She met him almost halfway and rubbed her flesh against him. It was a chore getting him to undress. He couldn't keep his hands off her, and when he did attempt to strip he was desperately clumsy about it. His tunic buttons gave him worlds of trouble. But Greta helped him, and finally he got his clothes off, and he touched her and she touched him and they kissed and Zvi swung.

The blow was a little off, landing on the top of the head. A few inches further back would have done the job better. As it was, the guard staggered but didn't go down. He started to cry out, and Greta wrapped her arms possessively about him and stopped his mouth with a kiss, and Zvi's second shot was in the right place, and out he went.

We waited a few moments, both for the sake of naturalism and to render the third guard so nervous and lustful that he would not notice how little Haim, who was donning the fallen guard's uniform, resembled his own comrade. Haim didn't return to his post. Instead he trotted straight to Ari, at the front gate, and called back to the remaining guard.

He, too, had learned a phrase or two of Czech. "Your turn. She could take on an army!" And then a description

97

of some of Greta's natural assets, quite accurate, actually.

By now we had the routine perfected. It took Greta only a few seconds to convince the third guard of the advantages of coeducational nudism. It took just one shot with the lead pipe to render him senseless. And now Gershon was dressing and taking up his post, and we had the game half won. Our armed Israelis held the three outside posts. I looked at them and thought what fine sentries they made. The Czechs had talked among themselves; Gershon and Haim and Ari stood straight and tall and silent. The Czechs had been bored by monotonous and pointless routine; Gershon and Haim and Ari were wholly fresh and alert.

The next part was tricky. Zvi and I moved up closer to the front of the castle. Greta put her clothes on again, and this time Zvi helped her with the various hooks and clasps. His hands wandered a bit far afield, and Greta's response told me that all of this was getting to her in a big way. I was worried that she might not be able to hold herself back one of these times.

We waited while she walked to the castle door. Gershon and Haim drew it open for her and she slipped inside. The two guards within challenged her immediately. She told them just what she had done so far, and what she had in mind, and invited them to decide who would be the first to participate. The guards seemed unwilling to believe it, until the trio out front chimed in reinforcement.

"Best piece of ass I ever had!" Ari called.

"She could take on an army," added Haim.

And Gershon said his sole Czech phrase. He would have blushed if he had understood it.

A few seconds later Greta rounded the corner with another guard in tow. This time she was not acting in the least. She hurried him out of his clothes, smothered him with kisses, and dragged him down on top of her. Zvi moved toward them with the pipe, but I motioned him back to give

98

them another few seconds. Then I nodded, and he clipped the guard perfectly, and the score stood at four down and one to go.

Zvi helped me tie him, then dressed in the uniform and returned to the castle. "You are terrible," Greta assured me. "You could have waited another minute."

"This is war," I said.

"I am going out of my mind."

"Take a cold shower."

"You are mad."

"Keep saying to yourself, *He's a Czech, he's a Czech*."

"What good will that do?"

"None at all."

I hefted Zvi's length of lead pipe. Zvi could speak a little Czech, and though his accent was heavy he could understand what was said to him. That was one of the reasons I had picked him for inside work. It was one thing to fool the guards on the outside, where the light was bad. It was something else to con the one inside and make him think this dark curly-haired Israeli was the same blond guard who had been with him for the past few hours.

So he played it safe. He opened the door, and the last of the guards said immediately, "Where the hell is Kliment?"

"Taking a leak," said Zvi. "The girl is waiting for you."

"It's no joke, then? She's really taking everybody on?"

"If it's a joke, it's a good one. You in the mood, or should I send her home?"

"Just think—right now my wife's sitting home waiting for me. When did they put you on this shift, anyway? Do I know you?"

Zvi eased out the door. "If you want to wait for your wife..."

"Don't be ridiculous."

When Greta had him stripped, I used the pipe on him. I hit him a little harder than I had intended to, and at first

I was afraid he was dead. I certainly didn't want to kill one of them accidentally, not after the argument I'd had with Zvi earlier in the day. He was dead set against going through the tying and gagging ritual and insisted we should cut their throats at the beginning and be done with it. "Dead men speak softly," he said, and I countered with the argument that these men, live or dead, would not be inclined to speak at all. "Alive, they'll be a help to us," I argued. "They won't want to admit how they were had, so they'll make up some elaborate lie. If anything, they'll wind up covering for us."

I checked the man's heart. It was still ticking, albeit weakly. I tied him and gagged him and got into his uniform. It was an almost perfect fit. I asked Greta how I looked, and she said I was magnificent.

I took a breath. Now the last stage of the operation, I thought. Now I would march into the castle, stride past my men, climb the stairs in the left rear tower, find some way to handle the one remaining guard who stood between me and Kotacek, and lead out the Butcher of Bratislava to face the death he deserved. And in a basement a few hundred yards away he would be tried and convicted and hung by the neck until dead. . . .

Oh.

I lowered my eyes, put my hand to my forehead. I had gotten carried away again. The Israelis, the Stern Gang oath, the smooth synchronization of the operation—it was all getting in the way. I'd almost forgotten one rather important point. I wasn't supposed to help them hang Kotacek. I was supposed to rescue him; I was supposed to get the bastard away from them.

How?

"Is something wrong, Evan?"

"Slightly."

"What is the matter?"

100

"Nothing," I said. I straightened up. "Put your clothes on," I said. "Then leave by the front gate. And take my clothes with you. I can't wear this uniform forever."

"Where shall I go?"

"Get a taxi," I said. "Have it waiting in front of the house where they're staying. Motor running and all. Got that?"

"Yes."

I kissed her. It was a mistake; she had managed to cool down for a moment, and now I had gone and put a match to her fuse again. "Oh, darling," she moaned, writhing against me. "Oh, just wait a minute or two, just stay with me for a moment...."

I eased her away. "We'll have time later," I said.

I shook hands with Ari and Gershon and Haim. Zvi came out to join us and asked if I'd had trouble with the guard. None, I told him.

"I have another plan," I said. "I think I can get the old Slovak butcher to cooperate with us. It will be easier that way than if we have to drag him screaming and kicking."

"But how?"

"I'll pretend I'm a Nazi come to rescue him."

"You, a Nazi? He'll never swallow it."

"It's worth a try. Listen." I lowered my voice. "There's a guard at the head of the stairs. I'll go up there and take care of him, then I'll get Kotacek out of his cell. As soon as you hear me on the stairs, all of you go limp. Collapse, fall down as if you're unconscious. I'll parade him right through here and out. As soon as we're out of here, take up your positions again. Give us five minutes, and then join us at the house."

"You think it will work?"

"I don't see why not."

"Good luck."

I went to the left rear corner of the building. The spiral

101

staircase was there, even narrower and more winding than I had pictured it. I climbed an infinity of steps and flung a salute to the guard at the top.

"What are you doing here?"

"Who were you expecting? Adolf Hitler?"

The guard laughed. "Come to relieve me? I wasn't due for relief for another hour. What time is it, anyway?"

"The schedule's changed. You didn't hear?"

"I never hear anything. I just watch this bastard sleep." He looked at me. "You're new here?"

"My first week of night duty."

"Dull as hell, isn't it?"

"Yes. Say, what's that?"

"Where?"

"There...."

He looked, and I used the pipe. It continued to surprise me, the ease with which a man could be rendered unconscious. The guard dropped without a sound. I fumbled through his pockets for a key to the cell, found it, opened the door, and maneuvered him inside. I didn't bother to tie him up or gag him. I would lock him in the cell on the way out and that would keep him out of harm's way.

The cell was small, barren, unpleasant. At the rear, below the tiny window, Kotacek lay sprawled on a sagging cot. He was sleeping with his mouth open. He was even uglier than his pictures—a wide face of sagging skin, pockmarks around the nose, a majority of teeth missing. He was sleeping in his clothes, a gray sharkskin suit with wide lapels that had been too long out of a cleaner's hands. His body odor wafted up from the bed at me. He reeked.

There was no time to spare, but at first I couldn't move. I could only stand at the side of the bed looking down at him. You've been rescued after all, I thought. It was impossible. It took a Nazi nymphomaniac and a quartet of Stern Gang assassins, but we've got you just about out of this little fix, Mr. Kotacek. Though right now I'm hard put to explain why any of us bothered.

I put a hand on his shoulder, shook him. He grunted and rolled away. I shook him again and spoke to him in Slovak. "You must wake up, Mr. Kotacek," I told him. "I've come to help you. I am Evan Tanner, of the Slovak Popular Party. I've come to save you for the honor and glory of the Fourth Reich."

His eyes opened. He stared at me.

"What is this? Who are you?"

I told him again.

"How did you get here? The guards..."

"They are all unconscious. Hurry—we don't have much time."

"I am a sick man. How can I hurry?"

The silly old wreck didn't even want to be rescued. "We must hurry. I will help you, Mr. Kotacek."

He got to his feet, swayed, caught his balance. He looked down and saw the crumpled guard for the first time. "You did this?"

"Yes."

"Ah." He smiled, and I reached for his arm to guide him out of the cell, and something happened to his eyes. They got a hard empty stare in them, and his mouth dropped open, and his hand started for his chest and stopped halfway there, and while I stood gaping at him, he made an odd sound deep in his throat and pitched forward onto his face.

I rolled him over. I put my ear to his mouth. He was not breathing. I listened to his heart. No heartbeat. I felt for his pulse. He had no pulse.

"Oh, wonderful," I said aloud. "Tremendous."

After all that work, the ungrateful son of a bitch had dropped dead.

103

10

Obviously I should have gone back to New York.

I knelt by the motionless form of Janos Kotacek and tried to figure out what to do next. I couldn't lug him down all those damned stairs. I couldn't go down without my Stern Gang comrades suspecting I was trying to pull a fast one on them. I could wish that I was back in New York, but wishing would not make it so. What was I supposed to do for an encore?

I looked down at the corpse of Kotacek, poked it with a foot. "You," I said, "are causing me nothing but trouble."

Whereupon the corpse opened its eyes.

"Go ahead," I said, dazed. "Nothing you can do will surprise me now. Get up on your feet, walk, talk. You're a zombie. I'm Baron Samedi. You must do as I say...."

He sat up, then struggled to his feet. "Where are we?"

"In Prague. In jail."

"Who are you?"

"Baron Samedi. Evan Tanner. Kilroy. I don't know."

"What has happened?"

"You died," I said reasonably. "And then I touched you with my magic foot, and, like Lazarus, you—oh. I see. I get it."

"I have these fits. Seizures."

"I'll just bet you do," I said. I understood it now. It was one of his several illnesses, his catalepsy, and I suppose I should have recognized it right away, but it had not worked that way. When someone has a very obvious coronary right before your eyes, and when he lies there bereft of pulse and breath and heartbeat, you don't review his medical history. You simply decide that he's dead and blow taps or recite the Kaddish or whatever.

But he was not dead. He had had a cataleptic seizure. A short one, fortunately. From what I knew about catalepsy, the fits could last for a few seconds or a few days or anywhere in between. I wondered how often he had these little things. Not too often, I hoped. I could just see myself, dragging him all over Eastern Europe, with him going limp and flaking out every little once in a while.

A shock could bring on a fit. So could a light flashing at the right frequency, or the right succession of musical notes monotonously repeated, or a sudden extreme change in body temperature. In this case, it seemed likely that the shock of my sudden appearance had done it. Whatever the cause, he had gone into a seizure and had now come out of it, and none too soon. He was alive, and now we had to get out of the castle.

I said, "Heil Hitler."

"Heil Hitler. Who—"

"Do you remember what I told you before?"

"No."

"My name is Tanner, Evan Tanner. I'm a Slovak Nationalist and an agent of the Fourth Reich, and I've come to rescue you. Do you understand that much?"

"I am not a fool."

"Good. The guards are unconscious downstairs. We have very little time. You must trust me and come with me, and I will get you back to Lisbon."

"How do I know I can trust you?"

"I thought you said you were not a fool."

"You could be trying to trap me, and then I will be shot trying to escape."

"Do you want to stay here?"

"No," he said gloomily. "I will come with you."

The guard on the floor was stirring. I gave him another love tap behind the ear and he went back to sleep. Kotacek followed me out of his little cell. I closed the iron door, locked it, and pocketed the key. I led him down the stairs. He came very slowly and clumsily, and I kept pausing and looking back to make sure he was still there. A turn or two from the bottom I coughed a warning to Zvi, and heard bodies falling in response. When we reached the foot of the stairs Zvi was crumpled up in a lifeless heap.

"He is dead?"

"Only sleeping."

"You should have killed him," Kotacek said. "The only good Czech is a dead one. Give me your pistol. I will kill him for you."

"We have no time."

"A pity."

The doors were closed. I opened them, and Kotacek walked through ahead of me, pausing to glance at Gershon on the left and Haim on the right. "Two more of the swine," he said. "You can always identify a Czech at a glance. See the characteristic shape of the skull? The cheekbones? Hah. Some day we shall put a plastic bubble over all of Western Bohemia and then we shall turn on the gas. Hah! Too much trouble to load them onto trucks. Too much trouble!"

He was a charmer.

We walked down the path toward the front gate. Gershon and Haim lay in their places, and Ari . . .

Where was Ari?

He should have been at his post at the front gate. I looked

107

to either side of the path and couldn't find him.

"Wait right here," I said.

"Is something wrong?"

"I have to check something."

"Are we safe?"

"Sure. Just wait here."

I left him at the gate and raced back to the steps. I bent down beside Gershon. In Hebrew I asked him what the hell happened to Ari.

"He went with the girl."

"With Greta? Why?"

"Why do you think?"

I sprinted back to Kotacek. If the damned girl had dragged Ari along because she couldn't keep her legs together for another half-hour, I would throttle her. She was supposed to have a taxi waiting at the curb. We had about five minutes on the Israelis—I knew they'd change their clothes and come after us the minute we were out of sight. She was supposed to be there, ready and waiting with a car. Instead she had Ari along for company.

I hurried Kotacek along. We passed through the gate and I let it swing behind us. He asked where I was taking him. To safety, I said. I was a hero, he told me. I would be rewarded. Perhaps he would make me his personal aide, and I could assist him with his correspondence. Would I like that? I told him nothing would please me more, and suggested he walk a little faster.

"I am walking as fast as I can."

"All right."

"You should show more respect to your superiors, Tanner. That is your name? Tanner?"

"Yes."

"What is your rank?"

"Pardon me?"

"Your rank. Private, corporal, sergeant—"

108

"Oh. Captain."

"Get us out of here safely and you will be a major. I solemnly guarantee it."

He was impossible. I wanted to tell him to cut the talk and save his energies for walking, but I didn't even bother to try. We crossed the street and headed for the house. Already they were behind us. Gershon and Haim and Zvi, back in their civilian clothes again, and coming through the gate on our trail.

In front of the house, just ahead of us, was a Russian-made sedan with the motor running.

I couldn't believe it. How had she done it? What had she done with Ari? Where had she found the car? It didn't matter. We just had time. They were on the other side of the street. We could duck into the car and be gone before they knew what was happening. . . .

Oh.

Greta was on the passenger's side. And seated next to her, behind the wheel, was Ari.

He rolled the window down. "Here's the car," he said. "I came back with Greta and she told me you wanted a taxi, but I got us a private car instead."

"Oh," I said.

"Ari is very clever," Greta said. "He knows how to start a car without a key. He used the tiniest piece of wire." *I couldn't help it,* her eyes added. *He just came along, and what could I do?*

And Ari said, "Why did you want the car, Evan?"

I looked over my shoulder. Gershon and Zvi and Haim were crossing the street, their faces aglow with comradely smiles. "For later on," I said, weakly, "when we all make our getaway."

"So we get the car head of time?" He nodded approval. "You are a good planner, Evan. Excellent."

* * *

109

Zvi did not want to hold a trial. I think he was still upset because we had not permitted him to kill the Czech guards. "What is the point of it?" he demanded. "We all know he is guilty. We all know we are going to hang him. Why have a trial?"

"Because it is a necessary procedure. We are not barbarians."

"Did his kind ever hold trials?"

"Would you place yourself in his class?"

"It is not the same thing."

"My dear Zvi, it is precisely the same thing."

"Bah." Zvi turned his back on Gershon, who had been upholding the principle of law and order. "You can see the folly of it, can't you?" he asked me. "Among other things, the butcher does not speak Hebrew. What does he speak? Slovak?"

A few other languages as well, I thought, but Zvi had given me an idea. "Only Slovak," I told him.

"So! How can we have a trial?"

"Evan speaks Slovak," Haim said.

"Do you?"

"Yes."

"Then we might as well have this farce of a trial. You will interrogate him, do you understand? We will give the questions, and you will repeat them to him and translate his answers for us. Is that all right with you, Evan? It should not take long."

"I'm willing."

"And then," Zvi said, "we take the rope and stretch his neck."

"Providing he is found guilty."

"You are joking, Haim."

"Well..."

We were in the basement. Kotacek, wholly incapable of understanding what was going on around him, sat in the same chair in which I had regained consciousness a night

110

ago. Greta was near the door motioning to me. I went to see what she wanted.

"I couldn't help it," she said. "He insisted on coming with me."

"I know."

"I couldn't get rid of him. I told him he should stay at his post, but he wanted to come with me. Do you want to change your clothes? I brought your clothes."

"I'll change later."

"You look very pretty in your uniform. At least we got the car, but it is no good now, is it? I am sorry. He wanted to make love to me; that is why he came with me. The one time in my life I had something better to do, and he wanted to make love to me!"

"It's all right."

"What do we do now?"

"We're going to try him."

"For what?"

"For killing Jews."

"Him. He couldn't kill a gnat. What is going to happen?"

"I don't know."

They were readying the scene for the trial. Kotacek's chair was moved to the far wall, four other chairs grouped in a semicircle facing him. I moved toward them all, scooped the pencil-beam flashlight from the table top. I hefted it in one hand and slapped it against the palm of the other hand.

"Talk to him," Ari said.

"What should I tell him?"

"Explain that this is a court of law, and tell him the charges against him...." He went on to give me a long message for our prisoner. "Make sure he understands what is going on," he added. "He does not look particularly intelligent."

I stood in front of Kotacek. "Be very calm," I said in Slovak. "Look only at me and do not say anything just now. We are in very dangerous trouble right now. These men

111

you see here are Jews." His lip curled in a sneer. "Don't say anything. Listen to me. You have to trust me. Nod if you understand." He nodded. "Good. If you cooperate, I think I know a way to get out of here. But you will have to do as I say. Do you understand?"

"If you are quick with your revolver," he said, "you can murder all of these Jewish swine before they know it."

Gershon touched my arm. "What did he say?"

"He says that he is sorry for whatever may have happened in time of war, but he was only following orders."

"They all followed orders," Zvi said. "This is a farce. Why is it that no one ever gave an order? Ask him if he signed the order consigning the Jewish population of Bratislava to Belsen."

I looked at Kotacek. "I have a flashlight in my hands," I said. "I am going to shine it in your eyes. You must look directly into the beam. Do not take your eyes off it for an instant. Do you understand?"

He nodded.

"He admits it?"

"He does. What else shall I ask him?"

I pointed the pencil-beam light at Kotacek. I moved the switch to the middle position, for sending code, and I worked the little button rhythmically, a nice steady tempo, flashing the light monotonously on and off, on and off, and keeping the beam directed right between Kotacek's eyes.

"Ask him about his role in the extermination of the ghetto of Spisska Nova Ves. And the ghetto of Presov."

I said, "Stare at the light, straight at the light, keep your eyes directly on the light."

"But what is the point?"

It wasn't getting to him. I flashed faster, upped the tempo. The frequency of the flashes was supposed to have something to do with it. I didn't really believe it would work, but I considered it a slightly more realistic prospect than

112

divine intercession, and without one of the two we were lost. Of course he would get a shock when they put the rope around his neck, but it might be too late by then. And it might not send him into a seizure anyway.

"Ask him if he also ordered the extermination of the Gypsies, and the Slovak Socialists, and of thirty-five thousand Ruthenians, and..."

I speeded up the frequency of flashes again as Haim completed his question. When I saw Kotacek's eyes glaze I knew I had him. I held the tempo steady, worked my thumb in and out on the flasher button, and his eyes rolled and his mouth dropped open and I had him, I had him. He tried to stand up and barely got halfway out of his chair before his hand flew to his chest and a moan escaped his lips and he pitched face forward onto the basement floor.

"What has happened?"

"It looks like his heart. Is he all right?"

I eased my way backward, away from Kotacek. I wanted to get out of the center of attention and put the flashlight aside before someone thought to wonder why I had been flashing it in his eyes. I could bluff it off as an investigative technique, but I was as happy not to have to do it. Meanwhile, they could examine Kotacek and assure themselves that he was good and dead.

"He is dead!"

"Are you sure?"

"You think I have not seen enough corpses to tell? No pulse, no heartbeat, no breathing. I would say that he has had a heart attack. Perhaps a coronary thrombosis, but I could not tell for certain."

"Not poison? All of them carry it, you know. A capsule of cyanide in a hollow tooth..."

"Cyanide leaves them with a blue face. I would say a heart attack, but who knows? It could be some other poison."

113

"So he has cheated the rope?"

"Does it matter? He is dead."

"But not by our hands, under sentence of our courts."

"Not under a Czech court either. And he died in our courtroom. Is that not the same thing?"

"It is not the same thing at all."

"Why not? Show me the difference."

"He had not been found guilty, sentence was not passed, and he was not executed. Otherwise"—palms spread sarcastically—"otherwise you are quite correct. Otherwise it is precisely the same."

"Then we shall continue," Gershon said solemnly. "The defendant no longer is required to play an active role in the proceedings—"

"Which is fortunate," Zvi said dryly.

"Please. His role is finished, as we have all heard his testimony. You will bear me out, Evan, that he has pleaded guilty to all charges leveled against him?"

"He did mention extenuating circumstances. . . ."

"But he admitted his guilt?"

"Yes, he did."

"Good. Now it is upon us to reach a verdict, and then to pass sentence. I vote guilty, for my own part, and advise the death penalty. Zvi?"

"This is absurd. Guilty, death penalty."

"Ari?"

"Guilty, death."

"Evan?"

"Guilty, death."

"Haim?"

"If I said twenty years in prison, what would you do? I'm sorry. Guilty and death, yes, by all means."

Gershon smiled. "You see? It is unanimous. The prisoner has been found guilty and has been sentenced to death. Sentence will be carried out now by means of hanging. You, Zvi, get the rope, and we will hang him from that

114

beam there just as we had planned. Ari, give me a hand with him. Evan..."

This was too much. He was alive, but they thought he was dead. So they were going to hang him anyway and kill him in the process. I felt it was time to assert myself.

"That is barbaric," I said. "We are not barbarians. We do not hang dead men."

"It is the sentence. Alive or dead—"

"Sheer nonsense. He was tried and convicted and sentenced; that is sufficient. He died while awaiting execution, perhaps of a heart attack, perhaps induced by remorse for his crimes"—that, I thought, would be the day—"or perhaps in fear of the retribution he so justly deserved. It does not matter. Our organization has been the instrument of his death acting in the name of the Jewish nation and Jews throughout the world, and that is enough."

"His kind buried living men. Why not hang a dead one?"

"We are not his kind."

It went on this way for a few minutes. I was arguing nicely, but I couldn't have carried them by myself. Surprisingly, it was Zvi who came in on my side. His enthusiasm was evidently confined to the execution of living persons; once an enemy was dead, it ceased to interest him. Between the two of us, Zvi and I carried the rest.

"But there is one thing we may do," Zvi added.

"What?"

"An old custom of our people. Do you recall in the scriptures when Saul slew his thousands of the Philistines and David his tens of thousands? Do you remember what was done to the fallen enemy?"

No one seemed to remember. I remembered, but said nothing.

"Evan, perhaps you know. You are from America, are you not? You know what it is that the American Indians did to defeated enemy tribes?"

"They scalped them," I said, "but I don't see—"

115

"This is similar. But our people have brought back as trophies something other than the scalp. An Indian might return to his village with the scalp of one of his tribesmen and no one would know the difference. But a Jew could not take this from another Jew, because another Jew would not have it to lose. You know what I mean, Evan, do you not?

I nodded.

And gradually it dawned on the others. "But we don't have a rabbi," someone objected.

"Fool, we don't make a *b'rucha* over him, either. It is not a religious ceremony. It is an act of military triumph. Who will do it?"

"My uncle was a *mohel*," Ari said, "but—"

"Then you may do it."

"Must I?"

"Don't you want to? It's an honor."

"The honor should be yours."

"Evan?"

"It was your idea. Go ahead, Zvi."

And so he went ahead. We rolled Kotacek over on his back—and I prayed that he wouldn't pick that moment to come out of his funk—and Zvi took down his trousers and undershorts and exposed him.

"Someone give me a knife."

Someone gave him a knife. Greta had joined our little circle and was pressing against me, watching the proceedings with excited curiosity. Her eyes never left the theater of operations. I thought that corpses did not bleed and wondered if cataleptics did. This one didn't.

So we crouched there, in a basement in Prague, and Zvi used the knife and, effectively if awkwardly, brought to completion the circumcision of Janos Kotacek.

116

11

"Evan darling," she said, "there are some things I do not understand."

We were alone now. Well, not entirely alone; Kotacek, snug in the arms of living death, lay motionless a few yards from us. But my fellow Sternists had left. With them on their way, I was able to relax for the first time. As long as they remained with us in the basement, I kept waiting for Kotacek to come out of his funk and get himself executed all over again. Once they had finished their experiment in surgery, I couldn't get rid of them fast enough.

And they were in no rush to be gone. Ari still had hopes of horizontal pleasantries with Greta, a thought which had apparently occurred to one or two of his comrades as well. Zvi was concerned about the disposal of the corpse. I insisted that it was dangerous for them to stay and selflessly assumed the task of tucking Kotacek's corpse into the gentle waters of the Vltava. They felt I was taking an unnecessary risk. "We can all do it," Zvi said, "and then we can all leave together in the car." I told him to take the car, explaining that I had to get Greta back to Germany. We clasped hands all around, and each of them kissed Greta with rather more than pure fraternal affection. "You must come to Israel," Ari insisted. "You will be truly welcome there, Greta."

She agreed that she would love to see their country. They all kissed her again, and felt her body against them, and remembered how grand she had looked, all soft and nude, in the arms of one Czech guard after another. I didn't think I would ever get rid of them, but, reluctantly, they left.

And we were alone, alone with Kotacek, and there were some things she did not understand.

"Don't worry about it," I said.

"He is dead."

"Yes."

"They were going to kill him, weren't they? The Jews?"

"Yes."

"I wondered what you were going to do. I thought you might have a plan, a good plan, but then all at once he died. It was his heart?"

"Probably."

"My father will be very sad to hear that. He was so proud of me, going with you on a mission of such great importance. He had hoped we would succeed, and now I must tell him of our failure."

She looked exceptionally appealing just then. There was a little-girl tone to her voice, a look of abiding innocence in her blue eyes. And that, incredibly, was the girl's chief quality—her innocence. No amount of furious and forbidden activity, whether sexual or political, could triumph over it. She remained, despite it all, a blonde and blue-eyed child.

"It was not a failure," I told her. "Not entirely."

"No?"

"Certainly not. Kotacek was in jail. He would have had a dreadful trial followed by a public hanging. We spared him that. Then the Israelis had him, the Jews, and he would have gone through another trial. And, unless we managed to save him, they would have hanged him. So instead what happened?"

"He died."

118

"He would have died anyway, sooner or later. He was an old man, a sick old man. At least he died easily. At least we managed to spirit him from under the noses of the Czechs, and then cheat the Jews of their revenge. We have not failed, Greta."

She looked at me. "Then I have done my part."

"Your part and more. You were wonderful at the castle, you know."

"Was I?"

"You were excellent. The guards—"

She giggled. "The poor men. The expressions on their faces, the strength of their desire. They wanted me very badly, you know."

"I know."

"To expect to make love and to get hit over the head for your troubles. They will wake up with headaches and with no pleasant memories. I thought perhaps we could wait until they had finished making love, and then knock them out."

"It would have taken too much time."

"Oh, I know, but it seemed more kind, don't you think?" She walked over to the fallen Kotacek. "Ah, but look what they have done to him. I had always wondered how it was done, you know? And if it was painful. Of course there can be no pain when it is performed upon a dead man, can there? What did they do with it?"

"They took it along."

"Back to Israel? Why?"

"As a trophy. Like a deer's head, or a stuffed fish."

"How odd."

"They got the idea from the Bible."

"Like the haircut for Samson?"

"A different part of the Bible."

"Oh. It is a shame you were unable to hypnotize him before he had his heart attack. That was your plan, was it not? And thus you made him look at the flashlight?"

119

"You noticed that?"

"Of course. And you were not translating what they said. I don't know Slovak, but much of it is like Czech. Some sounds are different. You were telling him to look at the light, were you not? It is unfortunate that it did not work."

"Unfortunate."

"Oh, Evan," she said. What was I going to do with her? She thought that Kotacek was dead, and that was just what I wanted her to think. She could tell her father and he would spread the word, and the Stern Gang would leak the news in Tel Aviv, and the more people who thought he was dead, the fewer would be looking for him. I couldn't keep her around and I didn't have the time to take her back to Pisek. What was I supposed to do with her?

She said *Oh, Evan* a second time, and I looked at her, first at her eyes and then at the rest of her. I remembered the way she had looked on the grounds of Hradecy Castle and the way she had felt in my arms in her father's house in Pisek. And I saw how she looked now, flicking her pink tongue over her lower lip, standing with shoulders back, breasts pressing against the front of the sexiest dress in Prague, legs longer than ever in high-heeled black pumps.

Something that had been drained from me by the tension of the rescue mission had returned to me now that the mission, or at least a stage of it, had been completed. And my eyes must have showed it, because she said *Oh, Evan* a third time, and took a quick step forward and was in my arms.

"You look pretty in your uniform," she said.

I kissed her.

"You would look prettier without it."

I kissed her again. She ground her hips into me, giggled, took a quick step back and out of my arms. "They have left mattresses all over the floor for us," she said. "Wasn't that considerate of them?"

120

"Very."

"Let me see how pretty you look without your uniform."

I undressed. She watched me with hungry eyes. Then she laughed again and turned her back to me. "Help me," she said.

I opened the hooks and unzipped the zipper.

"I have certainly had a lot of practice with this dress," she said, slipping it over her shoulders, stepping out of it, kicking it aside. "On and off, on and off, on and off. Do you dare to embrace me, Evan? Some Jew will hit you over the head just as you take me in your arms."

"I'll risk it."

"How daring!"

She came to me. I kissed her, and she pressed against me, and I did not even try to tell myself that she was a Nazi. We found a mattress and lay side by side upon it. I could see Kotacek out of the corner of my eye, so I turned a little until I could not see him anymore. I could see only Greta, and that was enough.

My fingers drew swastikas upon her breasts. She giggled, and her hands reached and found. "Just like the poor old Slovak," she said. "Just like the Jews. Ah, what have I done!"

"You have performed miracles."

"I have indeed. Oh, Evan..."

I held her and kissed her. Our flesh met. Perhaps I ought to take her along, I thought. Even smuggle her all the way back to America. Keep her around the apartment. How fine she was, and how soft and firm and warm, and how she moved, and what sounds she made...

Until, at the peak, the apex, the real nitty-gritty, her eyes rolled in her head and her whole body went bone-rigid and her mouth twisted and she tore the air with screaming. And then, just as suddenly, her muscles went limp and her eyes closed and the scream died and she very quietly passed out.

I could hardly believe it. I had never had quite that dramatic an effect upon a woman. Laughter, tears, sighs, moans, perhaps. But screams and unconsciousness...

And then, as I turned from her, I saw that it had not been all my doing. Kotacek was standing beside us, staring down at us. She must have caught a glimpse of him, alive and hovering, just at the moment of truth. It was no wonder that she passed out. It was, now that I thought of it, rather remarkable that she hadn't dropped dead on the spot.

"What is going on? Where are we? What happened to the Jews?" He was babbling like an idiot. "Who is this girl? What are you doing to her? What is happening to us?" And, stopping suddenly to look down at himself, where, now that his blood had again resumed circulation, he was slightly bleeding, *"What in the name of God has been done to me?"*

I was a long time calming him. He was purple with rage and white with fear all at once, an unholy color scheme for a human being. He was also, I decided, a thoroughly ungrateful son of a bitch. Here I had saved his life twice in one night and he was berating me as though I had done something horrible.

I kept explaining the whole thing to him. I had trouble getting past the curtain of blind rage, but gradually bits and pieces of what I was saying began to soak in.

"You made me have a seizure," he said.

"Yes."

"Why?"

"Otherwise the Jews would have hanged you."

"Why did you bring me here in the first place? Why take me from the prison only to bring me into a nest of filthy Jews?"

"I needed their help."

"Help? From them?"

"They helped me rescue you. I had to use them, and then I had to trick them to get you away from them."

122

"But look what they have done to me!"

"You won't miss it. And would you rather have hanged?"

"I have been mutilated!"

"But you're alive. And you can still devote yourself to the cause."

"That is true. You have performed a service to the Reich, Major Tanner. I will not forget that."

"I'm only a captain."

"I promote you. An on-the-field promotion." He smiled, but the smile didn't last. "The Jews escaped?"

"I'm not sure that's the right word. But yes, they're gone now."

"You let them go without killing them?"

"Yes."

"I suppose it could not be helped." He looked down at Greta. For a moment he simply stared at her, and then his gaze changed to something beyond simple observation. "This girl," he said, rolling the word lovingly on his thick tongue. "Who is she?"

"A German girl."

"Of course, what else could she be? Such purity of features, such true wholesome beauty. What were you doing to her?"

"We were discussing philosophy."

"Do not make jokes, Captain Tanner." He lowered himself onto one knee, peered intently at Greta's breasts. "Like cream," he said. "Like silk, like satin."

He reached out a hand to touch her, and I kicked it out of the way. He looked up at me, puzzlement and fury mixed in his eyes. "What is wrong with you?"

"Don't touch her."

"Are you mad?"

"I made a promise to her father," I said. "I told him I would not permit you to lay a hand on her." It was only fair, I thought, that I should keep at least one small portion

123

of the promise I had made to the crippled little dwarf. I had taken the fullest possible advantage of Kurt Neumann's hospitality, and I had not paid him back as well as I might have. If nothing else, I could keep the old Slovak's hands off his sweet and pure daughter.

"You talk as if she were a virgin," Kotacek said.

"In a way, she is."

"I told you, do not make jokes. And would she miss it? Look, the girl is unconscious. I am an old man. How often do I have a young girl like this? She will never know the difference. Never. Why begrudge me a moment of pleasure?"

I had always despised him. A Nazi, a racist, a collaborator, a quisling, a Judas—I had despised him from the moment the rotten mission had been assigned to me. But now he was turning my feelings to something more personal. Now I loathed him, not just for what he had done but for what he was. I should have let him rot in jail. I should have let the Israelis hang him. And now, mission or no mission, I felt like kicking his teeth in.

Instead I said, "There is simply no time. And besides that, I have given my word to a faithful National Socialist. Also"—pointing to his wound—"you will be sore there for some time. Several days at the very least. It would not to do irritate it, or to risk an infection."

He saw the point of that. He drew himself unwillingly away from Greta. At the last moment he looked as though he was going to reach for her again, to touch her breasts or loins. He didn't. If he had, I really think I might have killed him. I hated him very deeply at that moment. But he didn't, and my fury passed.

"What do we do now, Major?"

My title changed every minute. "We get out of here."

"There are friends in Slovakia who would shelter me. Shall we go there?"

"We'll see." I wanted to go to my friends, not his. "First we get out of Prague."

"And the girl?"

I didn't like the way he was looking at her. I covered her with a bed sheet. She seemed to have lapsed from coma into simple sleep. I put my ear to her lips, listened to her breathing. It was gentle and shallow. It sounded as though she would go on sleeping for a few hours.

"The girl will stay here."

"She lives in Prague?"

"No."

I began dressing, putting on my own clothes instead of the Czech guard's uniform. I wrapped up the uniform in a bed sheet and tucked the Czech's pistol into my pocket. I didn't want to leave anything incriminating behind, in case some officials entered the basement before Greta had a chance to get up and out. I didn't think this would happen, but I wanted to make it as safe as possible for her. It bothered me a little, abandoning her in Prague. Still, I was confident she would get out of it all right, either returning to Pisek on her own or finding a new life for herself in Prague or elsewhere. For all I know, she might decide to go to Tel Aviv. She might like it there. An endless supply of Jewish lovers, and a paucity of Rhine maidens to compete with her for their attention. I tucked a sheaf of Czech banknotes into her hand, gave her a parting kiss, and gripped Kotacek by the hand. On the way out, I picked up the pencil-beam flashlight and shoved it in my pocket.

"You used that before," he said.

"Yes."

"You made me look into it, and you blinked it into my eyes. And then after that I had a seizure."

"That's right."

"You made me have a seizure?"

"Yes."

"You are able to do that to me, just by blinking the light in my eyes? That and that alone makes me have a seizure?" I nodded. "Perhaps," he said, "we ought to leave that behind. After all, Major, we will have no further need of it."

"I'll keep it," I said.

By the time we left the house it was about an hour or so before dawn. The Prague streets scared me. I could see and hear plenty of activity over by the castle—official cars, bright lights. I took his arm and we headed in the opposite direction. I was beginning to wish I had parked our little stolen car where I could get my hands on it. It had seemed sensible to leave it at the garage, but now we were stuck without transportation, and every cop in Prague was hunting for us.

We had to make a run for it, of course. But we could not dash south and west on foot, nor did I want to attempt to duplicate Ari's feat and hot-wire a car. The escape needed time to jell, and time too for Kotacek to cool off a bit. At the moment the city would be sealed up tight. In a day or two the officials would be certain that he was either dead and buried or well out of the city and the country as well, and we might be able to move around without looking constantly over our shoulders.

I hated the thought of imposing again upon Klaus Silber. It would mean putting the old man in great danger. It would also mean abusing his hospitality by giving shelter to one of the tribe of men who had taken Klaus from a professor's chair and clapped him in Buchenwald. The alternatives had even less appeal. We could not stay in that basement—it was too close to the castle, it was known to Greta and to the Israelis as well, and if anyone was captured and talked we would be taken in no time at all. Klaus Silber's place was the best of several bad choices.

We took a taxi there—again, the best of two bad choices.

126

Walking would take too long and entail too great a risk. The taxi driver did not seem to recognize Kotacek. I played things on the safe side by giving him an address two blocks from Silber's house, and we walked the rest of the way.

"We can trust Dr. Silber," I told him. "But do not speak to him. Say nothing to him. Stay in your room and sleep as much as possible. Do you understand?"

"Silber. Another Jew?"

"Yes. It doesn't matter. He does not know who we are or what we are doing. He will cooperate. Just stay in your room and be quiet—"

"For a National Socialist, you know a great many Jews."

"You're lucky I do. Otherwise you'd still be in jail."

"Perhaps I would be better off. Will you take me to Lisbon?"

"Eventually."

"The Czech swine stole me from my own home. Can you imagine? They searched for my records but could not find them."

I too had searched for his records, albeit briefly. I had gone to Lison en route to Vienna, and while I was there I stole an hour or two to ride out to his home and have a look around. I hadn't found a thing.

"They will never find them. My records are vital, did you know that? But perhaps that is why you were sent to rescue me. The records and the funds, the Party leaders would want to be sure of those, eh? Perhaps they did not care about me at all."

"Your service to the Reich is the reason they sent me for you."

"And not the records? And not the money in the Swiss account? Hah. It does not matter. I cannot walk further. Are we almost at this Jew's house?"

"Just two doors more."

Silber came to the door in a nightshirt. I told him that I

127

had a man who needed shelter. He could have the same room the girl had been in, I added, as the girl was on her way out of Czechoslovakia now. My friend Klaus accepted this as he accepted everything else. He showed Kotacek to his room, then came downstairs to see me.

"My friend is very sick," I said. "He was in one of the camps during the war. It affected his mind."

"The poor man."

"He's completely lost touch with reality. He has decided that he is a Slovak collaborator, a Nazi himself. He prattles idiot slogans about exterminating Jews and others. A perfect transference."

"Not uncommon. Wish fulfillment, perhaps. One would rather be the conqueror than the conquered. You will take him out of the country, Evan?"

"In a day or two."

"Stay as long as you like. The poor man, such a way to wind up. And now the war is twenty years in the past, and still he has such scars on his psyche. You will stay here too, Evan?"

"I won't need a bed. I'll be out most of the time. But we will have time for some good conversations, Klaus."

"I hope so, my friend. And do not worry about your poor comrade. I will see that he eats and sleeps well, and I will not let what he says affect me. I will ignore his words, the poor old fellow."

Klaus would have liked to talk then and there, but I made him go back to bed for a few more hours of sleep. I took some food for myself—eggs, bread, cheese, a couple of cups of coffee. I tried to read some pamphlets he had lying around, but I couldn't concentrate. I was a little worried about Greta.

I left the house and walked back to the castle. Without Kotacek, it was not a bad walk at all. When I got there, the basement was empty. She had gone, taking her new

128

dress, her other clothes, and the money I had left for her.

I was relieved. If she was up and out, she would be all right. I had great faith in the girl's ability to survive. No matter where life tossed her, I was confident that she would land on her feet. And roll over onto her back.

12

We spent four days at Klaus Silber's place. While we were there I followed the Kotacek case in the Prague newspapers. The guards had put together a good story. According to them, several dozen men armed with machine pistols and hand grenades had come over the fences and dropped down upon them, capturing the castle and overcoming all resistance before a shot could be fired in defense. The papers made no mention of the nude condition of the guards. Either they had managed to untie themselves and dress before giving the alarm, or else the press decided to withhold that particular tidbit from its readers. At least one man hadn't put his uniform on, if only because I had not left it behind for him. I finally wound up stuffing it in a trash can downtown.

Then, the fourth day, the newspapers reported that "reactionary elements of the Stern Gang, composed of Israeli fascist terrorists" had announced the trial and execution of the Slovakian Nazi. The general tone of the article suggested that it was lamentable that Israelis had used gangster methods in so friendly a nation as the People's Republic of Czechoslovakia, but that, after all, Kotacek was dead either way, and certainly deserved it, and if nothing else Czechoslovakia had been spared the time and expense of a trial.

None of the articles had hinted at any connection between Kotacek and one Evan Michael Tanner. Indeed, I had not been mentioned at all. So by the fourth day I felt we were safe to make our move. They wouldn't be looking for us now. We would run into heavy trouble if someone happened to recognize us, but there was a lot less chance now that he was officially dead.

And we couldn't leave fast enough to suit me. The Butcher of Bratislava was a rotten companion and a boorish house guest. He completely ignored my instructions about keeping his mouth shut in front of Klaus, and several times he tossed out Nazi speeches that could have been trouble if our host hadn't been so well prepared for that sort of thing. "The poor man," he said each time, "the poor deluded old fellow. Those camps leave one horribly scarred, do they not?"

Another time, he keeled over spontaneously, without benefit of flashlight. I thought it was the catalepsy again, and was frankly grateful for it. But I happened to notice that he was breathing weakly, and that his heart was still beating, and then I remembered other aspects of his medical history. He was a diabetic and had been off the needle ever since his escape. It was miraculous that he hadn't gone into diabetic coma immediately. He was in it now, and I had to send Klaus rushing off to a druggist for insulin and a hypodermic needle. I guessed at the dosage, and wound up giving him too much, and succeeded only in sending him right off into insulin shock. We stuck a lump of sugar in his mouth to balance it off. It was a little like *Alice in Wonderland,* eating first from one side and then the other side of the mushroom, but we finally managed to straighten him out. Through it all, I wanted in the worst way to let him die and be done with it.

I stocked up on insulin and got Kotacek to tell me just when he had to have a shot and just how much the dosage should be. Then the fourth day came, and we were ready

132

to roll. I left the house and managed to find the gas station where I had left our car. I was a little nervous about reclaiming the car—if the police had spotted it somehow, they'd be quick to grab anyone who came for it. But it seemed safer to use a pre-stolen car, which the officials had presumably forgotten by now, than to steal a fresh one. I went to the station, and the car was ready.

"Some vandal must have been at it," the mechanic told me as I paid him. "Someone went to work on that engine as if possessed by devils. I had a difficult time with it, believe me."

He hadn't done that well, either, I discovered. The engine ran more smoothly but still sounded pretty bad. I wasn't sure how long I could drive the little thing without having a breakdown. It would only be safe as far as whatever border we crossed first, as you cannot get a car across a frontier without the proper papers. But we would worry about that when the time came. I'd be satisfied if the car got us safely out of Prague.

I picked up Kotacek, stowed his insulin and needle in one of the bridal couple's suitcases, took the flashlight and revolver along with me, and loaded Kotacek into the back seat of the car. He didn't like that. He wanted to ride in front with me. I convinced him that he would stand less chance of being spotted if he sort of slouched in the back. He didn't like it any better, but he put up with it.

Klaus wouldn't accept any money. He absolutely refused. "The poor old fellow," he said. "A convincing transference, yes? One would almost believe he is what he thinks himself to be. Do you think there is any possibility of curing him?"

I said I didn't think so.

"Then you do what you can to make him comfortable. For my part, I am only glad I could be of service. The poor old gentleman!"

133

I got behind the wheel. "Let's get out of here," my cargo grumbled. "The scruffy old Jew makes me sick."

We got out of there.

The exit route I picked was fairly close to the one I had worked out in Pisek. I drove almost due east at first, straight through Bohemia and Moravia and into Slovakia. The countryside became progressively more pastoral, the towns smaller and more provincial as we went along. He wanted to stop in Slovakia, no doubt expecting to receive a hero's welcome there. I didn't bother to tell him that there were blessed few Slovakian Nazis left in Slovakia. Most of them had been fitted with ropes around their necks when the Russians liberated the country in 1945. A few, like Kotacek, had gotten out in time. If he had announced himself in the streets of Bratislava, they would not have given a party for him. They would have found a rope and done the job once and for all.

"You must stop in one of these towns," he said. "We can get proper food here, good peasant food that sticks to your ribs. And the people know me. They will want to welcome me."

I kept on driving. "Later," I would say. Or, "There's a car following us. I want to make sure he doesn't get suspicious." Anything, just so he would shut up and let me drive.

He was no bargain. I figured to cut south and cross into Hungary around Parkan, then cut across to Budapest. From Prague to Parkan, the roads ranged from bad to worse. The total distance was only something like 250 miles, but I couldn't figure to average much better than fifty-five miles an hour. Kotacek cut our speed by almost a third. He was the worst traveler I've ever met. I was constantly stopping the car so that he could urinate, because he had all the bladder control of a six-week-old puppy. He complained constantly. Time after time he made me stop to buy him a

134

sandwich at a roadside restaurant. He expected to go into an expensive restaurant and sit at a table and gorge himself; when I explained that this was plainly impossible, he sulked and then retaliated by announcing his hunger whenever possible.

And when he wasn't making me stop the car, when he wasn't complaining about the roughness of the road or the way I drove or the cramped quarters of the back seat, when he wasn't doing any of these charming things, then he would talk. Some of his babble was Nazi theory—what the Fourth Reich would do, its present strength, the countries where it was gaining ground, the new faces of the movement. And the plans which would be eventually put into action. First, obviously, the ultimate extermination of world Jewry. But that was only the beginning. Next would come the depopulation of Africa. "Of course the world is crowded, Lieutenant Tanner." I had been severely demoted this time. "That is only because the strong races have not done their duty in respect to weaker races. The primitive inhabitants were wiped out in America, although it took centuries before their decline rendered them no longer a danger. The Australians moved somewhat faster against the Bushmen. They are dying out quite rapidly, as I understand it. But no progress at all is being made in Africa. On the contrary, the black races there become stronger day by day. But when the world is ours, we will show the world how to clean house. They will be cleaned out, an area at a time. As we level the forest, so shall we liquidate the blacks. Can you visualize the potential of a white Africa? Can you imagine it?"

All of this babble was fairly hard to swallow, but the rest was worse. I didn't really mind hearing him go on and on about things which I knew were not going to come to pass. It was when he started on past history that he got to me. He enjoyed reminiscing about his days of glory as

135

Minister of Internal Affairs during the war. I didn't want to hear about it, but that didn't stop him.

"The ghetto at Bratislav. The way they screamed when we sent them aboard the train. But we did not let them know where they were being sent. *A nice ride in the country*, we told them. *A pleasant trip in the fresh air*. Fresh air! The trains went to Auschwitz. First give them showers. Hah, gas! And then the cremations. The Germans were brilliant technicians. They designed these magnificent crematoria on wheels. That is what one does with human garbage. Turn it to ashes and plow it into the ground. So that it shall be as though it never existed."

It was too much. I turned the wheel, eased the car off the road, braked to a stop. I got a flashlight and turned to face him.

"What are you going to do?"

"You ought to sleep for a while."

"No! You cannot do it to me. I will not look at it. Major Tanner, you must be sensible. And you must obey orders. Put that toy away. Do you hear me? I order you to put that toy away."

"It's not a toy."

"Captain Tanner—"

I got him again. It didn't take me as long to find the right frequency this time, and I found out that it didn't matter if he looked directly at the light or not, just so it got into his field of vision. He fought it and lost. This time a few flecks of spittle appeared in the corners of his mouth, and his eyes glazed, and out he went.

That cut the stops. I didn't pull over again until we reached the border. I drove a nice steady thirty-five miles an hour—I could no longer get any better from the engine—and I was on the outskirts of Parkan by eleven in the evening.

He was still out when I stopped the car. This was his best fit to date and he showed no signs of coming out of

136

it. And that, I figured, could turn out to be a problem. It was going to be tricky enough getting him across the border when he was conscious. I had a French passport the description of which I matched not at all. Even so I was better off than Kotacek, who had nothing. Awake he would be hard to transport. Asleep he was impossible.

I left him in the car and walked through the little town to a point where I could see the border. It looked well patrolled. The Danube forms the border between Czechoslovakia and Hungary at that point. Further east, there's no natural boundary. I went back to the car and decided that we had a better chance over open land. I found a road that headed east and followed it until we could see the border fortifications—barbed wire seven feet high, a no-man's-land ditch about eight feet across, then another stretch of barbed wire, then Hungary.

I parked the car, walked toward the border. That particular stretch did not seem to be very heavily patrolled. I crawled up close to the wire fence and looked in both directions. No one. A sign warned me that the fence was electrified. I turned from it, then realized that it was considerably cheaper to post signs than to electrify a fence. I wished Gershon were handy, with a live cat to bounce off the wire. I went back to the car, got the jack from the trunk, returned to the fence, tossed the jack gingerly against the strands of wire. Sparks leaped all the hell over the place.

Which ended any ideas I might have had about cutting the wire, or climbing over it.

I drove back to Parkan, fully expecting a flat tire now that our jack was hung up on the fence. The tires held out, though, and so did the rest of the car. The border, I decided, was plainly impossible. Alone I might have considered tunneling under it or climbing a tree and diving over it, but with Kotacek along for ballast neither method seemed realistic. We would have to go straight on through. Shortcuts

137

were out. We had to make our play at one of the conventional checkpoints, and the one at Parkan was probably as good as any.

I stopped the car, hauled Kotacek out of the back seat and propped him up behind the wheel. I found an extra can of petrol in the trunk and used it to soak the back seat. I made sure the flashlight was in my pocket but left the revolver by the side of the road. Then I got in on the passenger side next to Kotacek and leaned across him to start the engine. I steered with my left hand and used my left foot on the gas pedal and got us going straight through town and right up to the border station.

There were a handful of cars there waiting to enter Hungary. I started to take my position at the end of the line, then swung the wheel hard right and put the gas pedal on the floor. The car leaped wildly off to the right like a startled tortoise. I twisted the wheel in the opposite direction, almost flipped us over, and then a telephone pole appeared magically in front of us and I took it full speed, dead center.

13

I had my hand on the door handle when we hit, and I threw the door open and got out fast. I stood for a moment, faking grogginess, and scratched a match quickly and flipped it at the back seat. Then I dashed around the car, opened the door on the driver's side, and hauled Kotacek out from behind the wheel. I very nearly missed getting to him in time. His feet were barely clear of the doorway when the gas in the rear seat caught up with the match and started to flame. I hauled him away from the car, bent solicitously over him, looked up to see a mob of officials and curious bystanders charging our way, and turned my attention again to Kotacek as our little stolen car burst into flames and exploded all over the place.

The rest was fairly easy. The border guards had the good grace to assume that I was in severe shock. They made me lie down, covered me with a malodorous brown blanket, and eased small sips of surprisingly good cognac into me. They examined Kotacek and shook their heads, and a gray-haired man carrying a doctor's black bag hurried through the small crowd, knelt down beside Kotacek, listened to his heart with a stethoscope, and turned to me. In Czech he asked if the poor man had had a bad heart. In Hungarian,

I said that my uncle had been ill for many years. *Heart*, he pantomimed, touching his chest. I touched my own and nodded.

They took us into the Customs shed, Kotacek on a stretcher and me walking with the assistance of two heavy-set and sympathetic guards. On the way I said, "Oh, my God, my passport" and started for the car. They restrained me. The car was almost entirely consumed by the fire, they explained. Evidently the gas tank had exploded. If my passport had been in the car, I could forget about it.

They gave me more cognac in the shed, and eventually I calmed down and was able to talk sensibly. I had come to Czechoslovakia to visit Uncle Lajos, I explained. He was a Hungarian but had been living here for many years. Now he was sick and was not expected to live very long, and I would visit him and together we would drive back to Budapest so that he could be reunited for a time with the rest of the family. And he had been driving perfectly well, except that he had complained of heartburn, saying it must be something he had eaten—here they nodded knowingly—and then he had slumped over the wheel, and the car went this way and that, and . . .

They were very sympathetic. All I had to do was call a member of my family in Budapest. Then, if someone would come for me, I could go home with him and take my uncle's body with me. I would have to fill out several declarations regarding my lost passport, and they would require fingerprints and other documentation, but they did not want to delay me. They were, all things considered, quite decent about the whole thing.

The declarations were easy enough, and there was no customs examination to speak of, as the only thing I was smuggling into the country was a flashlight. Kotacek's pockets were completely empty. They led me to a phone, provided me with a Budapest directory when I proved unable

140

to remember my own phone number—*shock, of course, the poor young fellow has had quite a shock*—and permitted me to dial the number of Ferenc Mihalyi.

A woman answered. I said, "Mama? This is Sascha. Is Uncle Ferenc home? There has been a terrible accident. . . ."

The woman, whoever she was, did not ask questions. A moment later a man took the phone.

"This is Sascha, Uncle Ferenc. I am at Parkan, at the border. There was an accident; Uncle Lajos had a heart attack and is dead. If you could come for me, you see the car was totally destroyed, they are holding us here until someone comes for us. . . ."

I was a bit inarticulate, and the guard took the phone from me and went through the whole thing with Mihalyi. I waited nervously. I had never met Ferenc Mihalyi, and for all I knew he would not even know my name, let alone recognize me. I had no code word to throw at him and didn't dare attempt to identify myself with a batch of Czech and Hungarian guards hovering around me. If he did the natural thing, if he told the guard that there was some mistake, that he had no nephew named Sascha, that he had no brother named Lajos, that everything was meaningless to him, then there was going to be trouble. Grave trouble.

But Ferenc Mihalyi was a conspirator, and conspirators constitute a marvelous breed of man. They do not need to have pictures drawn for them. They are able to read between lines even when nothing is written there. "Your uncle will come for you," the guard said at last. "He says that you are not to worry, that everything will be all right. He will arrive within the hour."

He arrived, as it happened, about forty minutes after the phone call. It was a rough forty minutes because there was simply nothing to do but wait, no way for me to do anything positive. All I could do was sit there and wait for something disastrous to occur. My mind supplied any number of pos-

141

sible disasters. Kotacek could suddenly sit up, open his eyes, and ask what was happening. Ferenc Mihalyi could turn out to be a fink, in which case the Hungarian Secret Police would have interesting questions to ask me. Someone could remember some unusual regulation which barred the entrance of corpses into Hungary, or the exit of same from Czechoslovakia. Any number of things could go wrong, and I think I anticipated just about every last one of them.

But at last a car drew up, and a tall man with a broad forehead and a neat gray moustache strode to the shed. I got to my feet. "Sascha," he said, and we embraced.

"Poor Lajos," he said. "His heart?"

"Yes."

"Well. We shall make arrangements for the funeral. Is everything set? You have your bags?"

"Destroyed in the car."

"It is nothing to worry about. Are there any more formalities or can we go now?"

There was nothing else to sign. The guards helped us load Kotacek into the back seat, and Mihalyi and I got into the front seat and drove off. I didn't know quite what to say to him, so I waited for him to get things started. He apparently had the same idea. We drove several miles in silence.

Finally I said, "My name is Evan Tanner, Mr. Mihalyi. I am of course a member of the Organization."

"Ah. Must we continue to transport that man's body, or can we dispose of him in a field?"

"We'd better keep him. He's not dead."

"Ah. I am not Ferenc."

I gaped.

"No, it is no trick. Ferenc was going to come himself, but he thought there might be trouble, that they could not possibly imagine him to be your uncle. He is, you see, only twenty-eight years old himself. A few years younger than you, I would guess. My name is Lajos, like that of your

142

dead uncle. Except that you assure me that he is not dead. May I assume also that he is not your uncle, and that his name is not Lajos?"

"You may."

"Ah. You have business in Budapest? Or is this merely a way-station for you?"

"We are going to Yugoslavia."

"I assume you have no papers?"

"None. They were . . . destroyed in the crash."

"A most fortuitous crash. Yes. It should be simplicity to move you and your dead companion into Yugoslavia. We Hungarians are rather good at negotiating border crossings, you know. We had considerable practice ten years ago."

"I imagine you did."

"A great deal of practice. Some of us, however, did not leave then. Ferenc feels that those who left were cowards. Or felt that way in the past. He was only a boy then, but enough of a man to destroy two tanks. And to join in our vow not to leave the country. Were you here then?"

"No."

"Your name is not Hungarian. You are American?"

"Yes."

"For an American to escape into Hungary is rather the reverse of the usual course of events. It is more commonly the other way around. You do not happen to live in New Jersey, do you? I have a family there."

"I'm from New York. It's close to New Jersey, of course."

"They send us packages. Food and clothing." He smiled. "If I give you their names, could you speak with them when you return to America? There are things one does not put in a letter. You could tell them that we have no great need of food and clothing. You could tell them to send guns."

Ferenc Mihalyi had an apartment in the old section of Budapest. He and his wife and two children lived in three rooms on the fourth floor of a drab red brick building nestled

143

among several other buildings, also of red brick, also drab. Tanya Mihalyi was slender and birdlike, with light brown hair and constantly amused eyes. No one my age had ever called her Mama before, she told me. If she liked it, Ferenc assured her, he would call her nothing but Mama in the future.

We ate chicken paprikash on beds of light egg noodles. Kotacek was laid out neatly on the Mihalyis' double bed. They found it difficult to believe he was really alive, but I belabored the point until they accepted it. I didn't want him emerging magically from his trance and scaring my hosts into heart attacks of their own. Greta had only fainted, but the girl had an exceptional constitution.

After dinner we sat drinking Tokay. It was around midnight. Ferenc wanted to know if I felt up to traveling some more. "Lajos will provide his car, and I will take you to the Yugoslav border if you wish. Or if you are tired we can wait until morning. Perhaps it would be best to wait until your friend is awake."

"It doesn't matter. I'm not tired, and he can travel as is, if you prefer."

"Perhaps it would be best to go now."

"Fine."

"Because," he explained, "it might not be safe for you to stay here for very long. And it is still much safer to travel by night than by day. I will drive you directly south along the banks of the Duna. It should not take us more than two hours. Lajos has a very fast car. It does not look so fast, but his son is a mechanic and has worked wonders with the engine. We shall leave"—he hefted his glass—"when we reach the end of the bottle."

We killed the bottle. Ferenc left the apartment, walked the few blocks to Lajos' house, and returned with the car that had brought us from the border. Together we carried Kotacek down three flights of stairs and loaded him into the back seat. The car was Russian-made and resembled the General Motors cars of around 1952. Lajos, I was told, had a good position in the Ministry of Transportation and Communication. His political sympathies and his activities in 1956 were not a matter of record.

The night was cool, the moon nearly full in the cloudless sky. Ferenc was an uneven driver, making up in sheer determination what he lacked in natural ability. He aimed the car instead of steering it, and he was more a tactician than a strategist; he would hurl us into hairpin curves with no prior planning, then figure out a way to keep us on the road. I was a while getting used to this, but eventually decided that there was nothing too precarious in what he was doing. It only seemed that way.

"The border will be nothing," he said. "There is a place in eastern Serbia near the Rumanian border. The guards there are all friends. There is a break in the fence; you can walk directly through. Will he be awake by then?"

"Perhaps."

"An odd sickness. It is hard to believe that he is not really dead. Suppose, in one of these fits of his, that he really died. How would you know?"

"I wouldn't."

"Perhaps he is dead at this moment, and we neither of us know it. Perhaps you will carry him all the way back to—where is it that you are taking him?"

"Greece."

"Perhaps you will take him all the way to Greece only to find that he has been dead all along. A joke on you, eh?"

It was a horrible joke. I changed the subject and we talked about some mutual friends, members of some of the Hungarian refugee organizations I belonged to in New York. This one had married an American girl, that one had finally won the right to practice medicine, another was homesick and talked constantly of returning to Budapest. We talked, and I tried not to consider the possibility that I had managed to kill Kotacek somewhere along the line, and that I wouldn't know for sure until his flesh started to putrefy. I could have done it in the car crash, of course. Perhaps the shock stopped his heart forever. Could a man have a coronary in the midst of a cataleptic fit? I had no idea.

But eventually, after about an hour in the car, Kotacek solved the problem for me. He woke up.

He was hungry and ill-tempered and had to relieve himself. Ferenc stopped the car and we let him out, and he staggered over to the side of the road and did what he had to do. Then he came back to the car and got into the back seat again. Everything ached, he told me. He was hungry, his head ached, his back was bothering him, and where on earth were we? I told him we were in Hungary, heading south.

Hungary! He was delighted. He had met Admiral Horthy and overflowed with admiration for the Hungarian fascist leader. The Hungarians had been staunch allies during the war, he told me. Good men and true. Of course there were strong partisan movements, vicious bands of Resistance fighters, but that was no doubt due to the long domination of Jews over the Hungarian peasants. Still, he remembered a time...

I gave him a shot of insulin, then fed him some sandwiches we had brought along in a brown paper bag. There was wine as well, but I did not give him any. I wasn't sure what effect it might have on his diabetes, or whether it would be good for his heart. He ate greedily, then insisted we stop again so that he could urinate once more. We did, and he did.

And, while he relieved himself, hunched over at the side of the road, Ferenc turned to me with an accusation in his eyes. "This comrade," he said. "Who is he, Evan?"

"A Czech fugitive. An anti-Communist."

146

"There are all manner of anti-Communists."

"Yes, there are."

"I understand Slovak. I do not speak it very well, but I can understand it. I know what the man was saying."

"I see."

"There were men of that sort in 1956. They would face the Russian tanks so that we might have the sort of Hungary we had under Horthy. Exchange one set of masters for another, Communists for fascists. I think I know the name of your friend. I had heard that he was dead, in Prague."

"Perhaps this is a different man."

"Perhaps. I do not think so."

Kotacek returned to the car. For the first time he took notice of our driver. Who was this man? I told him he was a friend who had helped us enter Hungary and who would now help us get into Yugoslavia. A Hungarian here, Kotacek proclaimed, and began to enlarge on the role of Hungary in the foundation of the worldwide Fourth Reich. Hungarians were good healthy Aryans, he announced, and he began to trace the history of the Hungarian nation, a Magyar band who had come westward just as other tribes had come to settle in Germany, in Slovakia, in all of the pure Nordic nations. I half listened to him while I watched the expression on my friend Ferenc's face.

"I do not like your friend," Ferenc said.

"You cannot dislike him as much as I do."

"Oh?"

"I have been with him longer. I make excuses for him— his age, the state of his health. But I have grown to hate him."

"And yet you save his life."

"There are reasons I cannot tell you."

"You do not share his beliefs?"

"God, no!"

"But you have your reasons."

147

I picked my words with care. "He can supply valuable information. He knows secrets that others would like to know. I have managed to convince him that I am the sort of man he is. That I share his beliefs. It shames me to be with him, it sickens me to have him for company, but I do what I must."

Ferenc spent several minutes digesting this. Throughout it all, Kotacek was talking in the back seat. We both ignored him. Finally Ferenc said, "I am armed, you know. I have a pistol."

"I did not know that."

"I took it for protection en route, and to give to you at the border. You yourself should not be unarmed. Then I had thought of using it to kill the Slovak, once I realized who he was. My parents were partisans during the war, you see. He takes me for a Hungarian fascist, this Slovak of yours, but you see he is quite wrong. I thought I might have to kill you as well, but if you are like him, I think I could do so without any bad feelings. Now I do not know whether to believe you."

"You know of me?"

"I do now. Not when you called, but while Lajos went for you I did some investigating. You seem to be one of us." He paused. "I am not going to kill you or your friend, of course."

"Do not call him my friend."

"Forgive me. I of course am not going to kill anyone; I do not preface acts of violence with small speeches. Instead I am going to forget the name of my back-seat passenger. I never knew his identity. He never once awoke, and I had no idea who he was. You understand?" I nodded. "And in return," Ferenc Mihalyi continued, "you must do me one favor."

"What is that?"

"You must never tell anyone that it was I who helped this bit of filth to escape. I will tell no one that he is alive,

148

and you will tell no one that I am partially responsible for his existence."

"Agreed."

"A hellish bargain. He should not be allowed to live."

"He is old, and sick. He won't live too long."

"He has already lived too long."

The rest of the trip was dreary. Conversation stopped entirely. Ferenc and I could no longer talk to one another. We had each of us shed portions of self-respect, and we wanted only to separate and forget the entire night. We had genuinely liked each other at the beginning. Then Kotacek had awakened and spoiled everything, and now we could not wait to be away from each other.

We reached the border. The trip took less than two hours, because from the moment of Kotacek's awakening Ferenc had stepped up the pace, careening around curves at seventy miles an hour, driving as fast as he dared and somewhat faster than I dared in reckless haste to divest himself of his passengers. I did not blame him.

We waited in the car, Kotacek and I, while Ferenc found the proper guard and made the proper arrangements. Then he came back for us and led us to the break in the fence. The guard had carefully deserted his post, as had his Yugoslav opposite number. They would return, Ferenc told us, in ten minutes. By that time we were to be across the border and well on our way.

Kotacek walked through first. Ferenc produced a small black automatic from his jacket pocket. For a moment I thought he might shoot Kotacek in the back. At the time I would not have stopped him. Then he sighed and presented me with the gun.

"You may need this."

"I hope not."

"Perhaps one day you will come back to Hungary, without such baggage as this."

"I hope to."

149

"You will be welcome with us."

"You are kind, and generous."

"The gun," he said. "Should the situation change, should you have occasion to kill the Slovak, I would be pleased if you saw fit to use the gun."

He turned without a handshake and walked back to his friend's car. I hesitated only for a moment, then crossed through the break in the Hungarian fence, walked twenty yards to my right, found the break in the Yugoslav fence and crossed into Yugoslavia. I looked at the gun, at Kotacek, and over my shoulder. Ferenc was driving back toward Budapest. I put the gun in my pocket.

With Kotacek I had played the earnest Nazi, with Ferenc the liberal anti-fascist revolutionary. I examined my own feelings, the hatred I felt for my sloppy, sickly loud-mouthed cargo, and then I thought of my speech in Pisek, my address to the Bund. How the words had leaped from my throat with a will of their own. How role-playing had carried me along.

I thought of the Red Queen's advice to Alice. *Speak French when you can't think of the English for a thing, walk with your toes turned out, and remember who you are.*

Remember who you are. It was not all that easy, and getting harder all the time.

14

There was a time when they described the Balkans as the patchwork quilt of Europe. Since then the Iron Curtain had descended and the Soviet army had dyed the old quilt a uniform shade of red. Yet Yugoslavia remained the old Balkan patchwork quilt in microcosm.

In a way, the nation was like a carefully assembled jigsaw puzzle. From a distance one saw only the picture which had been created, one of progress and peace and harmony, independence from Russia, industrial progress, increasing westernization, a burgeoning tourist trade, and so on. But closer up the cracks appeared. Closer up one saw that the whole was composed of an infinity of little oddly shaped pieces held precariously together. Croatians, Serbs, Slovenes, Dalmatians, Montenegrins, Bosnians, Hercegovinians, Macedonians, all carefully if tenuously interlocked in a pattern called Yugoslavia.

A delightful country.

We crossed the border near Subotica, in the Serbian province of Voyvodina. We passed southward through the country step by careful step, making more stops than a milk train, moving from one band of fanatics to another. In Subotica we were received by two old women, spinsters, sisters, who claimed to be vaguely but directly related to the last king of Yugoslavia. They were monarchists and prayed for the restoration of a Serbian king to the Yugoslav throne. They fed us, we bathed, and they summoned a great-nephew of theirs with a horsecart. He had no idea of our politics and didn't seem to have much understanding of his aunts' political ideas either, but he took us twelve miles down the road before dropping us off and turning back to Subotica. We went from the monarchist ladies to a trio of Bosnian anarchists, from them to some Croat nationalists, and so it went, all the way through the country.

It took us a full week to go something like four hundred miles, although we probably covered twice that distance, zigging and zagging, going up some mountains and down others and around still others. It would have gone faster without Kotacek, but then without him there would have been no reason to take the trip in the first place. I didn't mind spending the time, anyway. As I've said, I like Yugoslavia. I liked eating bits of roasted lamb around a campfire in the hills of Montenegro. I liked talking with bitter-eyed young men in dimly lighted apartments, on hillsides, in farm cottages. I liked everything but Kotacek, and I was getting to the point where I could put up with him. Not because he was becoming tolerable. Never that. On the contrary, he had become increasingly loathsome to the point where I hated him with a steady, unremitting hatred. His words could not bother me now, not once I got to the stage of complete hatred. His delaying tactics, his need for insulin, his constant grumbling, his just as constant urinating, his propensity for embarrassing me, all of this ceased to have any particular effect upon me. With or without them, I hated the man.

"What a trip we are taking, Major Tanner! And to think that our friends sent you so far just to save my neck. An old neck, too. Old and feeble after years of service. But

152

why do they send just one man? Hmmm? It is a question I have been asking myself. Why just one man? They could have sent an army of liberation. . . ."

Or he would decide that I was an army in one, and when that happened I would get a promotion. "The best thing that ever happened to you, Colonel Tanner, was when you came to my aid. Did you realize it at the time? Perhaps not, but it was your good fortune. Your very good fortune that you came to the rescue of Janos Kotacek. You have a future ahead of you now, Colonel. You will be my aide. My aide! You know what that means? You will live in my villa in Portugal. You will be constantly at my side twenty-four hours of every day. I have lived too long alone, Colonel Tanner. You see? It is not safe living alone. The Jews are everywhere, they never forget, and one must have a bodyguard. You will be with me night and day, my boy, and you will learn a great many things. Ah, the things I know! Matters which will be useful to you, Colonel Tanner, as you become of more and more importance in our movement. . . ."

I do not believe he said this purely out of enthusiasm for me. It was in the nature of a bribe, I think. He hoped that I would become so keen on the idea of serving as his flunky that I would work my head off to keep him safe and happy. I was already breaking my neck in the interests of his safety, and nothing could have persuaded me to try to make him happy, so he was wasting his words. He seemed to have an endless supply of words to waste.

Another of his favorite themes was his monumental importance to the Fourth Reich. His records could not possibly be duplicated. And it was not just his records, he assured me. There were also the funds he personally controlled. Certainly the Party leaders would not like to see that money go up in smoke.

What money? "Nothing I keep about the house, you may

be sure, Captain Tanner." My rank had dropped again; perhaps the question had been impertinent. "Money tucked safely away in a numbered account in Zurich. Money that no Jews or Communists can ever take away from us. Money earmarked for Party activities throughout the world."

How much money? I asked him that question more than a few times. It was not that he was evasive exactly, but that he gave me a different answer each time. The figures he gave me varied from a low of a hundred thousand Swiss francs to ten times that amount, a range in dollars of $20,000 to $200,000. I was sure it was closer to the top figure than to the bottom one. Twenty thousand dollars is a lot of money for an individual but a fairly small amount for an international political movement. I was fairly certain the funds he was talking about ran well into six figures, if in fact they existed at all.

The money gave me something to think about. I had to worm his records out of him once we reached Lisbon, but the records did not concern me personally. They were the bacon for me to bring back home to my nameless master. The money was something else again. I did not want to leave it for the Nazis, nor did I feel it ought to remain forever in the custody of a Swiss bank. The United States government, as represented by my anonymous chief, had no particular legal or moral right to it. It was at that point that I got a shade more interested in the job I was doing. Now, for the first time, it looked as though there might be something in it for me.

But that was the last chance I had to pump Kotacek about it. Because by then we were two and a half days into Yugoslavia, and shortly thereafter he did everything possible to get us both killed. Whereupon I fixed it so that he didn't talk to me again for a while.

• • •

154

It happened somewhere south of a town called Loznica. It was morning, and we were eating breakfast in a farmhouse with two men whose names I did not know. The four of us were talking. It was one of those conversations in which I was speaking Serbo-Croat with them and Slovak with Kotacek. It could have been safe enough. I knew he didn't understand a word of Serbo-Croat, and I never suspected that the taller of the two understood Slovak. But you can never take ignorance of a language for granted in that part of Europe. It is not safe, and I should have known better.

Our hosts were Serbs, very passionate Serbs. Their primary discontent with the national government stemmed from the fact that it was not wholly Serbian. They felt that Serbs and Serbs alone should run the country, and that those portions of Macedonia controlled by Greece should come under Serbian jurisdiction, along with considerable territory in both Bulgaria and Rumania. Pan-Serbian nationalism is old-fashioned but still has a certain charm for me, and I was seconding their arguments with just the right amount of Serbian zeal.

The problem grew from the fact that Kotacek thought our hosts were Croats. There is no logical reason why Croats and Serbs cannot get along together, but there are a number of historical explanations. The Croats are Roman Catholics, the Serbs Greek Orthodox. The Croats use the Latin alphabet while the Serbs employ Cyrillic. During the war, the Nazis exploited these differences to weaken the country by setting each group against the other. The experiment was not entirely successful; Yugoslavia was the first country in Europe to organize a Resistance, and the partisans gave as good as they got.

But some of the German puppet leaders did a lot of damage. The Croat leader, Ante Pavelic, organized his own SS and developed a final solution to the Serbian problem. Pavelic is supposed to have kept several bushels of human

155

eyes in his office. He is supposed to have referred to them as "Serbian Oysters." I don't know whether he did or not, or what he may have used them for besides display. It is not the sort of thing I care to dwell upon.

But while I was agreeing in Serbo-Croat that Serbia's claim to the Greek portions of Macedonia was unquestionably valid, I was also nodding my head in assent as Kotacek said something like this: "The Croats were grand allies, believe me. They had an outfit called the Ustashis. Good troops, stout-hearted fighters. Killed Serbs by the thousands. I knew Ante Pavelic well; he's in Argentina now as I recall. And another Ustashi leader, I don't remember his name, but I believe he lives in your country, in California. Or he died recently, I don't know, these are terrible times, all of the old men are dying. . . ."

One of our hosts, the tall one, the one who understood enough Slovak to get the gist of what Kotacek had just had the bad grace to say, drew a gun. And pointed it at us. And held it on us, to Kotacek's amazement and my distress, while he translated Kotacek's ill-advised speech into Serbo-Croat. At which point we had not one but two persons in the room who wanted to kill us, which made, with myself included, three who wanted to see the last of Kotacek.

To top it all off, he was shouting in my ear. "What is this? What is it all about? I thought these men were our friends. I thought they were Ustashis. Didn't you tell me they were Ustashis, Captain Tanner? Or should I say Lieutenant? Why is . . ."

I tried to explain. No one wanted to listen. The two Serbs were arguing over our fate. One wanted to kill us at once; the other wanted to find out more about us. We had come well recommended, after all. They wound up locking us in a windowless cellar, and there, with my trusty flashlight with its pencil beam, I put Kotacek once more to sleep.

When they came for us, reinforced with four more men

156

holding rifles, I talked as quickly as I knew how. "I make no apologies for my companion," I said. "He is a fool, a lout. You know that and I know it. I speak for myself. On July 23rd last year I donated twenty thousand Swiss francs to the Council for a Greater Serbia. The donation was made to an office in Paris, but there are men in Belgrade who will confirm it. Call Josip Jankovic. In Belgrade. Or get a message to him. The words I say to this scum with me are of no consequence. The words he says are of no consequence. You should know who your friends are. You must . . ."

I went on like that, and gradually they wavered, and finally they checked the story I had given them. It happened to be true, as they found out in due course, and ultimately they unlocked the cellar door and helped me drag Kotacek out of it. They thought he was dead, which pleased them no end. I saw no reason to change their minds on this score. I agreed that he was dead and convinced them, God knows how, that I had to take his body back with me. Since they had no particular use for his corpse they made no great objection. I was provided with a donkey and a cart and left that night.

So we got out of there with our skins. But Kotacek had done his best to sink our little ship, and he had certainly managed to scare the hell out of me. From that time on I did not give him a chance to screw us up again. I could not take the chance. For an old revolutionary, he had certainly forgotten how to keep his mouth shut. He simply could not be trusted, not with the infinite variety of hosts and helpers we had to make use of if we were going to get out of Yugoslavia.

From that moment on I kept him in his blue funk. Twice he came out of it, and each time I let him stay conscious just long enough to eat and drink and urinate and take his insulin. Then the light appeared and flickered in his red-rimmed eyes, and out he went again. He didn't much like it, but then he didn't have much chance to complain about it, either. He just stayed out, and he was better that way, much better.

15

We still had the donkey cart when we crossed into Greece, and Kotacek was still lying in the cart. So was I. Some bales of straw and bundles of vegetables were arranged artfully over us. A Macedonian named Esram drove the cart and used some of my money to bribe the border guards not to take too close a look at the cart's contents. The bribe was accepted, the cart was passed on through, and we were in Greece.

It might have been a difficult border to cross but Esram crossed it all the time. He did not feel he was actually passing across a frontier at all. He was a Macedonian, and as far as he was concerned he was simply going from one part of Macedonia to another. That one part was said to belong to Yugoslavia while another part was said to belong to Greece, this was a matter of complete indifference to him. Some day he fully expected to lay down his life in an attempt to end this state of affairs. Macedonians had been dying in this fashion since time immemorial, and Esram expected to follow in the wake of his ancestors. Meanwhile he was content to follow his trade, crossing from Yugoslavia into Greece and from Greece into Yugoslavia, while never once leaving his homeland of Macedonia, crossing and recrossing a border in which he did not believe while smuggling contraband for profit and friends for friendship.

"You know," he told me, "we have not forgotten you. In the village of Tetovo you are a hero."

In Tetovo I had unwittingly touched off a one-day revolution.

"The town is rebuilding," Esram said. "The government has sent experts to assist in the redevelopment, and there are new buildings to replace all that was destroyed. If you were to go to Tetovo today and tell the people that the time has come, they would level all the new buildings. You remember Todor, who died in the fighting? His sister expects a child and swears it is yours."

"She speaks the truth."

"That is good. I cannot go much further; I must return soon. We are a good distance from the border, but still in Macedonia."

"Is it far to the train?"

"There is a train in Naousa. Twenty, twenty-five miles."

"If you will ride that far with me, you may have the donkey and cart. They are of no use to me now, and if you do not mind the trip you may take them back with you."

"I cannot pay for them, my friend."

"I meant you to have them as a present."

"You are kind. But you can sell them profitably in Naousa. The animal is old but still in good health, and the cart is sound. You might realize as much as—"

"I do not need money; I have more than I need. And I would want the donkey to go to a man who would treat her kindly, and not abuse her. She has been a good companion."

"Better than the one in the back, eh? More lively?"

We laughed. He pulled out a goatskin pouch, wadded up tobacco, crammed it into the bowl of a cracked old pipe. He lit it and smoked and called in Macedonian to the donkey. Domestic animals in that part of the world must answer and respond to a wide variety of languages. What he now told the donkey was, "Keep walking, nice little donkey, and I

160

will take good care of you." Whether the animal heard or not, she most assuredly kept walking.

"She is evidently a Macedonian donkey," Esram said. "See how nicely she obeys?" He laughed again. "I will be glad to have her. You are kind. And I will treat her well."

At the railroad station in Naousa I bought two tickets for Athens. When the train came Esram helped me carry Kotacek inside and sit him upright in a compartment. "Too much wine," we explained to a passing conductor. "He is old now. He cannot handle it the way he used to."

"My wife's father was the same way. He will not vomit?"

"No."

"That is good."

Along with the donkey and cart, I gave Esram my pistol, the pistol I had received from Ferenc. He had expressed the hope that I kill Kotacek with it, but that was not to be. "A gun for Macedonia," I told Esram. "I know you will put it to good use."

"I will treat the donkey with kindness and the gun with respect."

"And here." I gave him a variety of currency—Czech bills, Yugoslav bills, even some Austrian notes. "I don't know how much this is. Someone can change it for you into dinars. Give it to Annalya, for the child when it is born. Tell her I think of her often. Tell her...you will think of things to tell her. Tell her I will come back some day."

"She knows."

The train was slow, bouncy, boring. Kotacek and I were alone in our compartment for most of the way. Fortunately we were still alone when he came out of his fog.

"Where are we?"

"Greece."

"The Greeks are pigs. When we are in power—"

161

I put him out again. It was almost frightening how perfectly it worked.

Athens was the end of a long road. The Iron Curtain was rusted mesh, and we had wormed our way through it. There would be no more stolen cars, no more donkey carts, no more trains. In Athens we could obtain passports, and from Athens we would fly directly to Lisbon, and that would be that. I was about ready to do something the easy way for a change. I was tired, thoroughly exhausted.

Kotacek came to in the railway waiting room. I had managed to wrestle him off the train, again passing him off as a drunk, but I didn't want to cart him all over the city that way. I put him on a bench and sat down beside him. I read a newspaper and waited for him to come to. The Greeks never bother a man who is reading a newspaper. No one bothered me, and I sat there for an hour and a half and read every word in that newspaper before Kotacek finally woke up.

I took him in turn to a restaurant, a lavatory, and the home of an Armenian moneylender named Sarkan Besmoyan. Sarkan and I had corresponded extensively for many years. Although we had never met before, I felt I knew him well enough to ask him to recommend a good passport artist, and he evidently felt he knew me well enough to oblige me. He gave me an address in the Turkish quarter.

I left Kotacek with him. "Please do not permit him to leave your house," I said. "His family is worried about him. He is an old man and gets confused easily. I am to bring him back to his friends and family, and if he wanders about harm may come to him."

"He is safe here," Sarkan assured me.

I had a great deal of trouble finding the passport artist. First I couldn't find the street, and then it developed that Sarkan had given me the wrong house number, 86 instead of 68. I finally found my man, a thin withered Turk with bad teeth and cloudy eyes. I told him that Sarkan Besmoyan had sent me, and that I required two American passports.

"Impossible," he said. "I can let you have one."

"I need two. How long a wait would there be?"

"An infinite wait. Perhaps forever." He rummaged through a drawer and produced a blank passport. "Do you see this? Do you know what it is?" I did, and said no. "This is a reject. Do you see? The imperfection in the cover? When blank passports are produced, a certain number are rejected. They are destroyed. Except that in certain instances they are not destroyed, and instead they find their way to Athens. Or to Beirut—there is a gentleman in Beirut who obtains quite a number of them. But a good many come to Athens, to me. I pay very well for them, you see."

"I see."

"The production of a counterfeit passport is no simple matter. You see all of these lines in the paper? The intricate pattern? One cannot very easily draw in all of this. One is far ahead of the game when one has a blank passport at one's disposal. Then one types in the necessary information, punctures a false passport number into the cover and first three leaves, attaches a photograph, impresses photo to paper with a duplicate of the Great Seal of the United States— but you do not want to listen to all of these details; that is not what you came for, eh?"

"It's very interesting."

"It is also profitable. I must charge five hundred American dollars for such a passport. If I had two of them, one thousand dollars. But I do not have two of them. To be honest, I must say that you are lucky I have one. Will British do? I have never been able to obtain blank British passports, but I have several stolen specimens. It is not a simple matter to remove the inks and photographs and substitute the proper data and a more suitable picture. And there is the added

163

disadvantage that all of these passports have no doubt been reported stolen. The numbers are thus on file. The chance that someone will notice this is negligible, I grant you, but it exists."

He went on in this vein for some time. I learned a great deal about the business of a passport forger but not very much about how Kotacek and I were going to get back to Lisbon. I finally wound up buying two passports, an American one for myself and a Brazilian one for Kotacek. I managed to get the pair for seven hundred fifty American dollars. It was the first good chance I'd had to spend the expense money I'd been given, and I didn't really mind parting with it.

I gave the passport forger my name, age, height, and all the rest. I told him what entrance and exit visas to mark in the appropriate places. I still had my vaccination certificate, and from it I read off my passport number—F-886852.

I went back to Sarkan's house, collected Kotacek, took him to a passport photographer and had our pictures taken. I dropped him back at Sarkan's and took the photos to my forger. He put them in place and forged the proper seal on mine. In essence, I had managed to replace my own passport with an identical duplicate of it. The one the Czechs had taken from me—the one they had taken from my little French friend, to be precise—was now reborn from the ashes. True, it had cost me $500, but it seemed easier than going through channels.

The thought of Fabre reminded me that I still had his passport. I fished it from a pocket and offered it to the forger. He could always use French passports, he said, and would gladly pay me fifty dollars for it. One hundred, I suggested. We settled on sixty-five.

I took money and passports and left. Mine was perfect, good enough to carry me anywhere. I felt a good deal better having it in my possession; I could walk through the streets of Athens without the feeling that at any moment some policeman might tap me on the shoulder and ask for identification.

But I still didn't feel very good about Kotacek. He was, according to his passport, a Brazilian national named Pedro Costa. But could he speak Portuguese well enough to fool them at Lisbon immigration? And could he refrain from speaking Slovak or German? And could he keep his mouth shut all the way? And, worst of all, would they by any chance recognize him? The Portuguese had certainly heard a lot about Kotacek recently. The abduction, the scheduled trial, the disappearance—it stood to reason that they might have published his photograph in the newspapers from time to time, and that the men in the customs and immigration service might well have seen it, and even studied it. If he was recognized, the game was up.

I went back to the house. He was waiting for me, delighted to see me. He intended to take a little nap, he informed me, but first he wanted me to see about getting him something to eat. I did, and he ate a hearty meal and had me poke some insulin into him.

"I have made a decision," he said. "We are not going to Lisbon."

"Oh?"

"We go instead to the United Arab Republic. Think of it—would it not be absurd for me to return to Lisbon? The Czechs know my address there. They would make another attempt to abduct me."

"But they think you are dead."

"So let them think so. It would not do for me to reappear there. No, we will go to Egypt. Have you ever been to Egypt? Cairo is a beautiful city, very modern, very clean. We..."

I was sure I could talk him out of it but I didn't even try. Because he would only talk himself into it some other

165

time. And he would speak German to the stewardess and Slovak to the immigration officer, and everybody would recognize him, and he would shout "Heil Hitler" at some inopportune moment and deliver one of his little speeches about Jews to some Hassidic rabbi, and all the way, while I worried about all the embarrassing things he might do, he would talk and complain and boast and eat and drink and urinate.

The past week had spoiled me. I was used to having him unconscious, and now I had to contend with a wide-awake Kotacek all the way from Athens to Lisbon. It would be several hours' worth of maneuvering him through situations in which he would have to maintain a front for the benefit of others. I was not at all sure he could do it.

"Listen," I said, "just tell me where to get my hands on your records. Then maybe you can go on to Cairo after all, and I'll go to Lisbon—"

"Ha! No, I think not. We will both go to Cairo."

I hadn't really expected that to work. I picked up his Brazilian passport and had a look at it. It wasn't terrible, but it wasn't the most perfect work in the world, either. If you held it so that the light hit it just right you could see where some of the writing had been removed and a new inscription added. It didn't look too great right around the photograph; the original photo had been just a shade larger, and it looked funny there, as though someone had messed around with it, as indeed someone had.

These were minor flaws, and I didn't think they would matter much in the normal course of events. Immigration officers and customs inspectors see hundreds of passports every day, and I doubt that one in ten thousand is a phony. So why should they look for it? A passport normally rates a glance and nothing more.

Unless something attracts their attention. And Kotacek seemed a good bet to attract attention. If only I could put him out, if only he could make the trip in the corpse-like state that I found so infinitely preferable to his real self. Alive, he was a pain. Dead, he was good company.

But there was a difference between palming him off as a drunk on a milk train from Naousa to Athens and playing the same game on an international airline.

Unless...

I left the house and took a cab to the airlines terminal. I bought a pair of tickets to Lisbon. Lufthansa, the German line, had the best schedule, an early evening flight with no intermediate stops between Athens and Lisbon. I bought two tickets in the tourist section, one for Evan Tanner, one for Pedro Costa.

That night Kotacek went to sleep an hour or so after dinner. He seemed to need a great deal of sleep. Ten hours at a stretch during the night, and always a nap or two in the course of a day. Between this and his cataleptic fits, it struck me that the man might as well be dead. He only got to use a few minutes of the day anyway.

I stayed up with Sarkan. We played several games of backgammon, all of which he won, and did some not too serious drinking. We drank ouzo, which is one of the things I cannot drink too much of. Sarkan gave up eventually and went to bed, and I stayed downstairs reading and sipping coffee through the night. When dawn broke I went up to Kotacek's room. I found my flashlight and sat in a chair next to his bed waiting for him to wake up.

When he did, he got the light in his eyes. Flicker flicker flicker, and back he went to dreamland.

I let him lie there for a while. Then, when I heard Sarkan moving around in the kitchen, I hurried downstairs. "You'd better call a doctor," I said. "My friend seems to have had a heart attack."

"Is it very bad?"

"I think he's dead."

167

• • •

The doctor was an Armenian and an old friend of Sarkan's. He came in a hurry, rushed to our patient's side, examined him at length, and began to massage his heart. That worried me—suppose it worked? But it didn't, and he didn't think to cut open Kotacek's chest and try a fancier method of heart massage. He confirmed that Kotacek was dead, and wrote out a certificate of natural death which testified that Pedro Costa had died of coronary thrombosis.

They were very understanding at the airlines. They sent me to the proper officials and had me fill out the proper papers. Mr. Costa had died in Greece, and of course I would want to ship him back to Brazil for burial. No, I explained; he was a Brazilian citizen, but had originally lived in Portugal and would want to be buried in his family plot in Lisbon. It was all arranged. He would fly on the same plane with me, the Lufthansa flight that very evening. There would be no problem.

They refunded the difference between tourist passage and the fee for shipping a corpse, which turned out to be considerably less costly. With the difference I bought a sturdy pine box. I had the box delivered to Sarkan's house where we loaded Kotacek into it. I was a little worried about how he would travel. If the luggage compartment was not pressurized, he might get himself killed in there. I wasn't sure how it would work. And, if the luggage was not secured some way, he could get badly knocked around.

I called Lufthansa and asked them about it, explaining that I would not want the corpse disfigured. They were understanding again. There was no danger, they assured me. The compartment in which he would travel was fully pressurized and quite comfortable. After all, it was what was used for transporting pets, dogs and cats and such, so it had to be safe.

That helped. It covered all the bases but one. There was still the possibility that Kotacek would come to somewhere between Athens and Lisbon, in which case we were in worlds of difficulty. No one would hear him bellowing down there, but there was a good possibility that he would suffocate.

I waited as long as I could on the chance that he might come to before flight time. He didn't. I nailed the lid on his coffin—not too tight, in case he did come to—and called an undertaker who sent a hearse to convey the coffin to the airport. At the Lufthansa flight desk his passport—stamped DECEASED—and his death certificate were attached to the coffin lid, along with several other official documents whose precise function I did not wholly understand. I was sent into a waiting room, and the coffin was placed on a conveyor belt which would take it, presumably, to the plane.

It was an excellent flight, not too crowded. I had a vacant seat next to me, the one I'd previously reserved for Kotacek. I leaned back and enjoyed the flight. One of the stewardesses reminded me slightly of Greta.

We caught a tailwind and landed fifteen minutes early. I breezed through Customs—I had no luggage at all by now, so that was no problem—and collected Kotacek from the appropriate depot. They didn't have a hearse handy, so I had to rent a whole limousine. I gave the driver Kotacek's address. When we got there, the two of us carried him inside and set him down in his living room. I waited until the limousine was long gone before I opened the coffin.

He was just as I had left him. But, I thought, suppose he had awakened? He would have suffocated. And, suffocated, he would look just as he looked now. I would never be able to tell the difference. I could only wait and see what happened. If he came out of it, he was alive. If he began to spoil, he wasn't.

169

16

By the middle of the second day in Lisbon I was fairly certain he was dead. He had never been out quite this long before. I had him stretched out on his bed, and I was beginning to regret having taken him out of the coffin. I'd only have to stuff him back into it and call the undertaker.

But I was sufficiently exhausted to appreciate the rest. I spent almost all my time sitting around the house and doing next to nothing. I left once, to stock his kitchen with food, and one other time, to buy a strobe light at a photo supply shop in downtown Lisbon. The rest of the time I did as little as possible. I listened to fado music on his radio, took long glorious baths in his tub, cooked and ate small meals in his kitchen, drank port wine and black coffee and Spanish brandy, and loafed around while my body unwound and my nerves came back to normal. I hadn't realized at the time what a strain the whole business had been. I had been on the go twenty-four hours a day for too many days and I badly needed a chance to loosen up a little.

When I wasn't bathing or loafing or listening to records or eating or drinking, I searched his house. His records, after all, were what I had come for. If I couldn't find them, I might as well have let him rot in jail. They might have been easier to find if I had known just what I was looking for. I didn't. They could be anything from a set of ledgers to a spool of microfilm. I went over the house from top to bottom. I took up the carpet and looked under it. I checked for loose bricks in and around the fireplace. I moved pictures to search for hidden wall safes. I did all of the things they do in the movies when they are hunting for something and a few more besides, and I got nowhere.

The fourth day, he came in from the cold. I was downstairs and heard him bustling around up there. I went up to see him, and there he was at the head of the stairs with a gun in his hand. I'd come across the gun in my search, a little .22 caliber item in the bedside table. Now it was pointed at me.

"Easy," I said. "Take it easy."

"We are in my house in Lisbon."

"Yes."

"How long have we been here?"

"Just a few days."

"A few days." He looked at me, then at the gun. He still had it pointed at me. I didn't really think he was going to shoot it, but I wasn't sure.

"We were supposed to go to Cairo."

"It was impossible."

"Why?"

I had had four days to prepare my answer. "There is a war going on there," I said. "Israel has invaded Egypt. The government has fallen. It seemed unwise to go there now. At the last minute I managed to cancel our plane reservations and book passage here."

"A war."

"Yes."

He shuddered. "You were wise, Colonel Tanner. Of course you should have consulted me first." He lowered the weapon, came down the stairs. He looked, I saw, much the worse for wear. Loose folds of skin hung from his face.

His eyes were bloodshot, rimmed with massive circles. He looked like a man who had stayed up all night, not like one who had been sleeping for four days like a corpse.

In the living room he suddenly discovered the pine box. "What is that?" he demanded. "It looks like a coffin."

"It is a coffin."

"What is it doing here?"

"I had to ship you in it," I said.

"In that thing?"

"Yes. From Athens to Lisbon."

"In that thing? In a coffin? Me? In a coffin, like a corpse?"

"Yes. There was no other way."

"I could have sat in a seat like a human being—"

"You had one of your seizures. Don't you remember?"

"But you did that to me. The flashlight—"

"Not this time. You had the seizure yourself. In fact I thought it was a heart attack, and a doctor pronounced you dead."

"And then I rode in a coffin." He shuddered violently. It was too vivid a glimpse of his own mortality, and he didn't like it one bit. That shudder of his was damned real. Then he got hold of it and turned it into a laugh. "In a coffin!" he said, now delighted with the idea. "A joke on them all, eh? A fine joke." He set the gun down on a table and rubbed his hands briskly together. "Well, we are home now. Perhaps this is better than Cairo, after all. Well, I need a bath, a shave, and some food. You will draw my bath, please. Not too hot but not too cold either. Then while I bathe and dress you may cook something. You can cook? Of course, I am sure you can, Captain. . . ."

We were home now, and I was his aide, all right. And his orderly and valet and man of all tasks. I drew his bath and laid out soap and a razor for him. He certainly needed a shave. His beard had gone on growing while he was in his fits. This had led me to assume he was alive, until I

173

remembered that the beards and fingernails of corpses continue to grow for a while after death, another thought I didn't care to hold onto for any length of time.

While he was washing himself and shaving, I cooked him a big meal. I wanted plenty of food in him because I had the feeling that the next few days were going to be rough ones for him. I wanted him in good shape. I'd worked out the methods I'd have to use to get the records. Winning his confidence wasn't going to make much difference—he was still in command, he was the general and I was the lieutenant or captain or major or colonel, depending upon his mood, and he wasn't about to turn his records over to me. I had to break him, and break him good. And I had had plenty of time to find a way to do it.

I fed him six eggs and five strips of bacon and plenty of toast and coffee with cream and sugar and some sweet rolls and everything else that I could find that he could eat. He was full of compliments for my cooking. He wiped his mouth and belched and wiped his mouth again and trundled off to the bathroom. When he came out I was in the doorway waiting for him. I didn't bother with the flashlight this time. I had the strobe aimed right in his face, with the flashing mechanism set to just the right frequency. He got one step out of the bathroom and collapsed into my arms.

I took him back to the bedroom, stripped him, stretched him out on his back and tied him up neatly, spread-eagled, his feet and hands fastened with thin cord to the bedposts. I hadn't wanted to knock him out again but I couldn't think of a better way to get him in position and set the stage. I didn't expect he would be out too long, anyway. His usual stretch was only a few hours, and the four-day blackout he'd just had was atypical. If it took four days, I would just have to wait.

I set the stage the way I wanted it. I masked off all the windows and the door so that not a ray of light entered the

174

room. I set up the strobe light so that it flashed not into his eyes but off to the side, and I set the frequency way below the level that knocked him out. It flashed quite slowly, on and off, on and off. I found a small record player downstairs and pawed through his records until I found one of Nazi marching songs. It was a 33 rpm recording, and I set the player for 45 rpm. I turned off the strobe because it was bothering me, and I sat in the darkness and waited for something to happen.

Nothing did for a very long time, perhaps six or seven hours. Then I heard him breathing, starting to stir. I leaned over and flicked on the strobe light and let it flash monotonously on and off. I turned a dial on the record player and the "Horst Wessel Lied" began to play, pitched too high and played too fast. I kept my hand on the volume dial and made it now louder, now softer, now louder, now softer.

He discovered his bonds. He called out for me. He wanted to know what was happening, why he was tied, where he had been taken. I did not make a sound or move a muscle. I stayed very still on the dark side of the room while the light flashed and the crazy music played on and on.

After a while, maybe fifteen minutes although it seemed like an hour to me and must have constituted a week of subjective time to Kotacek, I began to vary the frequency of the flashes. I still kept them way below the blackout range, but varied the flash speed enough to turn his world a little further inside out. He was getting hysterical now. I didn't want to overdo it. He was supposed to have a bad heart, and I was putting him through a special kind of hell.

Finally I began to talk with him. The two of us had always spoken in Slovak, so I avoided that language at first. I cupped my hands around my mouth to make my voice hollow and as weird-sounding as possible, and I talked to him in German.

"We must have the records. You must tell us where they

175

are. The Fuehrer wants your records. You must find the records. Where are the records? The Fuehrer needs the records. . . ."

I broke that off after a while, moved to another part of the room and hit him with Spanish. He had a working knowledge of that and of Portuguese as well, and I kept pitching at him in both of those languages, then shifting gears, working in German again, returning to Slovak, pitching my voice a little differently each time.

I had him reeling. I kept it up long past the point where I myself was thoroughly bored with it, and then I cut it all out at once, the talking, the flashing, the music. I turned off the record and cut the strobe and sat down in the darkness. He didn't make a sound at first. Then I heard him making a sort of clicking noise. I couldn't figure it at first, and then I got it. His teeth were chattering.

A few minutes later I got things going again. I pitched the strobe at a different part of the room where I'd drawn a large black swastika on the wall. I set the speed down low, so that a beam of light would illuminate the swastika on the white wall for about four seconds, then there would be four seconds of darkness, and then the light again, a nice boring pattern. I slipped noiselessly over to the side of the bed and whispered in his ear.

I told him he was on trial, that he was going to be killed. I begged him to confess so that his life would be spared. I kept on in this vein, over and over. He asked what he had done, what he was supposed to confess to, where he was, who was going to kill him. He was just filled with questions. I pretended that I did not hear anything he said. I talked on over his words, switching languages constantly, often in mid-sentence. I asked the same questions over and over again, and then I began to intersperse the questions with others. The location of the records. The number of his account in the Swiss bank. The name of the bank. At one

176

point I very nearly had him. He told me the name of the bank, the Zurich-Geneva Bank of Commerce, and then he stopped cold. "Tanner!" he shouted. "What in God's name are you doing to me? What is it? What do you want?"

He was oriented again, and I was worried. But I was fairly sure it was going to work. He had let one part of his guard slip. He had mentioned the name of the bank. The rest would come in due time. He knew who I was and knew where we were, but he would lose the thread before long. The music and the voice and the flashing had to get him sooner or later. I think it would have gotten anyone, sick or healthy, young or old. I'm sure it would have gotten me.

He never recognized me after that. I kept it up, the mixture as before, constantly changing it, constantly keeping it the same. The first thing I got was the bank account number, then the current balance. It was about what I had guessed, just over half a million Swiss francs, or about $130,000 U.S. I jotted down the account number and some other scraps of information, and when I was done I had enough to get the money out of that account and into my own numbered account at the Bank Leu.

It would take a trip to Zurich, and perhaps require some false identification and a copy of Kotacek's signature, but it could be done. On the way home or at my leisure. Already I was portioning out the money in my mind—so much to Hungary, so much to Israel, so much to Macedonia, to Ireland, to Kurdistan, to Croatia. And some, no doubt, to the girl in Macedonia who expected my child. And perhaps a bit to Kurt Neumann, and surely some to Sarkan's friends in Athens, and . . .

But I still had to find the records. I turned my attention to Kotacek, squirming in his little homemade hell of Nazi march music played off tempo and a light that flashed on and off, on and off, illuminating a black swastika on a white wall.

It didn't take very much longer. He coughed it up in

bitter gasps and he cursed around the words, cursed the Jews and the Czechs and the Negroes and the Orientals, cursed all the persons and peoples he blamed for the miseries of the world, all of which miseries had suddenly come down around his head. The words poured out in a bitter stream of Slovak, a river of black slime. I couldn't listen to him. I fled from the room and went down the stairs to the living room. There was a false drawer in his desk. The drawer's bottom was composed of two pieces of very thin wood artfully fitted one atop the other. I took the fittings of the drawer apart and slipped out one of the pieces of wood to expose the meat in the sandwich, a dozen sheets of onionskin covered with careful, tiny writing. Part was in Slovak, part in code. The part I could read was enough to convince me that I had found the bacon. This was what they wanted in Washington. They were welcome to it.

I went back upstairs. He was roaring now. I turned off the music. I got the stobe light, and pointed it not at the wall, not at the swastika, but at him. His face was drawn, his eyes wild. I set the frequency of the strobe up to the right level and let him have it. His eyes swallowed up the magic flashing light as if hungry for the blackness it would bring, and his face relaxed in mock death as he went out and under.

I put out the strobe light, turned on the light overhead. I went to the window and removed the black paper and masking tape. Outside the hot Portuguese sun was shining. Before I had not known what time it was, whether it was night or day.

I stood for several minutes at Kotacek's bedside. I had gotten what I came for, what I had been sent for. The records for my pudgy string-puller, the money for whomever I decided to give it to. And a filthy old Nazi, a pathetic old Nazi, had been saved from the rope. No trial, no execution.

He could go on living, writing his letters, weaving his webs of intrigue, bolting his food, injecting his insulin, worrying about his heart, and periodically, tasting false death in a cataleptic fit. He could go on in this fashion for a year or two years or five years or more, until one time the seizure was permanent and the death real.

I thought over my mission and decided that I did not like it very much. I should not have saved him from the Czechs, who had a right to kill him, or from the Israelis, who had an equal right to put him in his grave. And I could not make myself believe that saving him was of such monumental consequence to the United States of America, or that a living Janos Kotacek made for a better world.

I had not even improved Kotacek's situation. I looked at him, a creature of fits and palpitations and gall and urine, and thought how much better off he would have been at the end of a rope. The Israelis had whittled off a piece of him, and the trip from Prague to Athens to Lisbon had shaved him smaller, and now I had turned his mind inside out and picked his brains. God alone knew what he would be like when he came out of the fog this time. What would he remember? And what would be left of him?

Only an excess of hatred kept me from wasting pity on the man. "You have lived too long, and to no good purpose," I said aloud, and turned and walked from the room.

17

When I got back to New York I went straight to my own apartment. There was a note from the post office. I'd had too much mail for the box to hold, and would I please come down and pick it up. I called them up and told them they could damned well deliver it, since that was what the senders had had in mind when they put stamps on my mail. They grumbled but sent it over, three big sacks of it. I dumped everything out on the floor and spent two days just sorting the stuff, trying to determine what to read first. I was just getting to the point of opening and reading various letters when the telephone rang. A girl asked if this was the Rutledge Coat-Checking Service. I said it wasn't. But wasn't this TRafalgar 4 1114? No, I explained, it wasn't TRafalgar anything, it was seven goddamned numbers, and I didn't like it any more than she did, and I suggested she join the Anti-Digit-Dialing League. I hung up and went back to my mail, and it was half an hour later before I got the message.

The Rutledge was the hotel where I'd met him the other time. 1114 was his room. Coat-Checking Service sounded like Kotacek, and I'm sure some bright-eyed young genius spent three weeks of government time thinking up that one and another week patting himself on the back. What was left? The telephone exchange. TRafalgar 4. Meet him at four o'clock? Probably.

181

I stopped at the desk on the way in and asked the aging faggot room clerk the name of the party in 1114. "Nelson," he said. Sure, why not? That explained the TRafalgar. They were worse than hog butchers in Chicago; they used the squeal and all.

He opened the door for me, led me inside, made drinks for both of us. He looked exactly as he had looked at our last meeting. The suit was different, a gray one this time, also expensive, also ill-fitting. We found chairs and sat down and looked at each other. I waited for him to start it. He, after all, had called me.

"You're here," he said at length. "And on time. The girl who phoned you was afraid you might not have understood the message. Said you made some flip reply, as though she had really called the wrong number."

"I didn't want to interest anyone tapping my phone."

"Of course. That's what I told her." He worried the ash on his cigarette. "I know most of what happened this trip, Tanner. I suspect we can call the mission a qualified success. To be quite frank, I don't think anyone else could have done as well. You got the man out of prison. That in itself was remarkable. And I can think of no better end for him than having him abducted and killed by Israelis. Keeps the U.S. out of it entirely, and puts our friends in Czechoslovakia in rather a bad light. As though the Jews *had* to get him themselves, don't you see, because otherwise the Czechs would have let him off too easily. Instead of the fun and games of a war criminal trial, they came off looking like a bad joke. Like the brunt of a bad joke."

I didn't say anything.

"I'm sorry he had to die. And sorry he died without getting his records to you. Though, to be honest again, I never expected much in that direction." He smiled humorlessly. "I didn't actually expect to see you again, either."

I didn't say anything.

"I don't know if you have anything you wanted to report, Tanner. But if so, now's the time."

I still didn't say anything. I opened my briefcase and took out Kotacek's notes and handed them to him. It took him a few seconds to figure out what they were. When he looked up his face was a study. Coat-Checking Service indeed! If he wanted to play games, I had the bat and the ball, and he had a hole in his glove.

"Where did you get these?"

"Kotacek gave them to me. In Lisbon."

"But the Stern Gang—"

"Thought they had killed him. They didn't."

"How did you manage that?"

"I tricked them."

"You tricked them." He put out his cigarette and freshened his drink. "You tricked them," he said again. "That's incredible. And then you got Kotacek back to Lisbon, where he turned the records over to you. So we get the information, and we also get a nice official-but-unofficial version going around which lists Kotacek as murdered in Prague by Sternists. This gets better and better. We have the best of both worlds, do you see? A live Kotacek whose secrets we know, and an officially dead Kotacek, and—" He sipped his drink. "I don't suppose I should ask how all of this came about. It's incredible good luck for us. Does Kotacek still think you are a Nazi? Does he know that you've taken this information? Of course"—shuffling the papers—"these are all originals, not copies. He'll miss them, and no doubt that will tip things. Unless he actually gave these to you? I—"

"Kotacek is dead."

"But—oh, I see. He died in Lisbon."

"Yes."

"His heart, I suppose?"

"No." I hesitated a moment, then decided the hell with it; it served him right for giving me assignments. I didn't

183

want to be his boy wonder. I wanted to be left alone, and if he heard this all the way through he would leave me alone for all time. He might slap my wrist for acting without a double-o number or whatever, but that was all he would do to me, and he certainly wouldn't come knocking on my door with orders to rescue any more grubby Nazis.

"No," I said, "it wasn't his heart. I murdered him."

When I left Kotacek's room that day I went downtown and found a man named Afonso Carmona. I told him what I wanted and he in turn told me something I had not known.

"What you seek is illegal in Portugal," he said. "This is a Catholic nation, you know, and the Church prohibits such rites. I assume your friend was not a Catholic?"

"No."

"Come inside, please. We can talk better in private." We went into a cold, dark room. "There would be many persons in attendance?"

"Only myself."

"Ah. Completely private, then."

"Yes."

He stroked his smooth chin. "Then it is more nearly possible. I do not have the facilities myself, but there is a friend of mine, a colleague. He cannot do this thing openly, but if you will wait I will call him. Is that satisfactory?"

"Certainly."

I waited while he made the call and chatted amiably but discreetly with his friend. He wrote out the name of the friend's establishment and place of business. He took my address and said that he would see that a car and driver was sent to me in an hour's time. I thanked him and took a taxi back to Kotacek's house.

He was still out cold. I undressed him, put his best suit on him, and dragged him all the way downstairs again. The pine box still rested on the living room floor. I got him into

184

it and nailed the cover shut. I had just finished when the hearse pulled into the driveway. There were two helpers plus a driver, and the four of us got the coffin loaded and headed for the funeral parlor.

On the way I thought of one of Kotacek's little speeches. *"The ghetto at Bratislava. The way they screamed when we sent them aboard the train....First give them showers. Hah, gas! And then the cremations. The Germans were brilliant technicians. They designed these magnificent crematoria on wheels. That is what one does with human garbage. Turn it to ashes and plow it into the ground. So that it shall be as though it had never existed...."*

He had written his own epitaph.

The death certificate written in Athens was still on the coffin. The undertaker studied it, looked over the passport, then raised the coffin lid to examine Kotacek. "He is well preserved," he commented. "Dry ice?"

"Pardon?"

"When he was shipped here, he was packed in dry ice?"

"Oh. Yes."

"I thought so. Of course they cushioned his face so that it would not burn the skin. Very well done. Now with cosmetics we could improve his appearance if this were to be a regular funeral, but for a cremation you would not want to bother, would you? I thought not. And there are no other mourners?"

"No mourners."

"Then we may proceed."

I told it all just the way it happened. How they put him in the oven, pine box and all, and how a few hours later I left the funeral parlor with the ashes in a paper bag. When I finished, neither of us said anything for several minutes. He poured fresh drinks for both of us, and we both seemed to need them.

Finally he said, "What on earth did you do with the ashes?"

"I thought of plowing them into the ground, but it seemed an excess of metaphor. I eventually threw the bag in a garbage can."

"Mmmmm. Appropriate, I suppose." He lit another cigarette. "You killed him."

"Yes."

"Had him burned alive."

"Yes."

He thought about it some more. "Actually," he said, "we may be better off with him dead, the more I think of it. The Nazis'll assume he died in Prague and that we never did get to his records. Which is just as well, their not knowing what we know, that is. Of course we did pick up a lot of bits and pieces through him, but the stuff you came back with is more important by far. Yes. Yes, I think we're in better shape with him dead."

"I think the whole world is."

"How's that? Oh, yes." He put out the cigarette, looked at me. "I should be irritated, shouldn't I? You took matters into your own hands. Made a moral judgment and acted upon it. You were ordered to keep him alive, and yet you killed him. In spite of orders. Against orders."

"Yes."

"I should be angry." He got up and walked to the window. To the window he said, "But I'm not angry, Tanner. Not even mildly irritated. I'm not entirely certain why that is. I'm a poor administrator, I'm afraid. I *like* men who take matters into their own hands. And who act upon their moral judgments. It'll be a hell of a day when we all turn into machines. A godawful day." He turned to face me. "You know something, Tanner? I'm *glad* the son of a bitch is dead."